PUFFIN BOOKS

ROUND THE CHRISTMAS TREE

All the warmth of a traditional Christmas, complete with
log fires and mince pies, is here in this marvellously varied
collection of short stories for young children.

From the enchanting flow of the traditional stories, like
Alison Uttley's *The Fairy Ship* and *The Big White Pussy-
Cat* (retold by Leila Berg), to the preposterous comedy of
H. E. Todd's *Another Mince Pie*, this is a splendid mix of
magic and laughter which makes a perfect book for reading
aloud round the Christmas tree.

Sara and Stephen Corrin are the editors of many popular
anthologies for children, including *The Puffin Book of
Modern Fairy Tales* and *Once Upon a Rhyme*, which are
both published in Puffin.

ROUND
THE
CHRISTMAS
TREE

EDITED BY

SARA AND STEPHEN CORRIN

ILLUSTRATED BY JILL BENNETT

PUFFIN BOOKS
IN ASSOCIATION WITH
FABER AND FABER

Puffin Books, Penguin Books Ltd, Harmondsworth, Middlesex, England
Viking Penguin Inc., 40 West 23rd Street, New York, New York 10010, U.S.A.
Penguin Books Australia Ltd, Ringwood, Victoria, Australia
Penguin Books Canada Ltd, 2801 John Street, Markham, Ontario, Canada L3R 1B4
Penguin Books (N.Z.) Ltd, 182–190 Wairau Road, Auckland 10, New Zealand

First published by Faber and Faber Ltd, 1983
Published in Puffin Books 1985

Made and printed in Great Britain by
Cox & Wyman Ltd, Reading
Filmset in 11/14 Linotron 202 Aldus by
Rowland Phototypesetting Ltd, Bury St Edmunds, Suffolk

CONTENTS

Contents

ACKNOWLEDGEMENTS

We are grateful to the undermentioned publishers and authors for permission to include the following material:

'The Big White Pussy-Cat' from *Folk Tales* by Leila Berg, first published by Brockhampton Press, now Hodder & Stoughton Children's Books.

'Father Christmas and the Carpenter' from *Mrs Pepperpot Again*, and 'Mrs Pepperpot's Christmas' from *Mrs Pepperpot's Year*, by Alf Prøysen, published by Hutchinson Publishing Group Ltd.

'The Fairy Ship' from *John Barleycorn*, and 'The Little Fir-Tree' from *Mustard, Pepper and Salt*, by Alison Uttley, reprinted by permission of Faber and Faber Ltd.

'The Christmas Train' by Ivan Gantschev. Copyright © 1982 Bohem Press, Zurich. English edition published by Frederick Warne (Publishers) Limited, London, 1982.

'Father Christmas's Clothes' from *The Tin Can Beast and Other Stories* by Paul Biegel, translated by Patricia Crampton, published by Glover & Blair Ltd.

'Schnitzle, Schnotzle and Schnootzle' and 'The Voyage of the Wee Red Cap', from *The Long Christmas* by Ruth Sawyer, are reproduced by permission of The Bodley Head.

'Schnitzle, Schnotzle and Schnootzle' and 'The Voyage of the Wee Red Cap' from *The Long Christmas* by Ruth Sawyer. Copyright 1941 by Ruth Sawyer. Copyright renewed 1968 by Ruth Sawyer. Reprinted by permission of Viking Penguin Inc.

Acknowledgements

'Another Mince Pie' from *Bobby Brewster's Balloon Race* by H. E. Todd, first published by Brockhampton Press, now Hodder & Stoughton Children's Books.

'The Naughtiest Story of All' from *My Naughty Little Sister* by Dorothy Edwards, published by Methuen Children's Books.

'Winkle and the Christmas Tree' from *Lucky Dip*, by Ruth Ainsworth, Penguin 1981. Reprinted by permission of the author. .

'The Way of Wishes' by Jean Chapman from *The Sugar-Plum Christmas Book*, Hodder & Stoughton (Australia) Pty Limited, 1977.

'Lotta's Christmas Surprise' by Astrid Lindgren, published by Methuen Children's Books.

'Lotta's Christmas Surprise' by Astrid Lindgren, by permission of A. B. Rabén & Sjögren Bokförlag, Stockholm.

'Miss Anna Truly and the Christmas Lights' by V. H. Drummond, reprinted by permission of the author.

'Wag-by-Wall' by Beatrix Potter is reproduced with the permission of the publishers © copyright Frederick Warne & Co. Ltd.

Our thanks for their readiness to help at all times are due to: Margaret Hazelden, Children's Librarian, and Hazel Wilkinson, colleagues at Hertfordshire College of Higher Education; Mary Junor, Schools Librarian, Barnet, and all her kind colleagues of the Barnet Libraries; and Jan Mudford, Children's Librarian, Swiss Cottage.

The generous advice and guidance of Phyllis Hunt, Children's Books Editor at Faber and Faber, and her team, have, as always, been invaluable.

FOREWORD

Despite the romantic presentation of the scene on the traditional card with the well-fed, too red robin, the whiter than driven snow and the excessively scarlet holly, it is the warm hearth and the tree with its pretty lights and baubles that draw the family together to celebrate the festival of the year.

With toys unwrapped and explored almost to breaking point, with plum pudding and turkey vying for the attention of the digestive juices, what can be more agreeable for a child than to snuggle up to a friend or relative and listen to a tale about Christmas in other homes and other lands? In fact, wherever children are gathered, in schools, libraries and any Christmas event or celebration, the exciting and memorable experience of everybody enjoying a story together will be an essential part of these festivities.

The stories in this collection – *Round the Christmas Tree* – are dramatic and reassuring enough to leave the listener with a warm, glowing feeling, just right for the season of good will.

They are intended mainly for small children, though it may be claimed that they have enough meat to attract children of all ages.

LEILA BERG

THE BIG WHITE
PUSSY-CAT

Once upon a time there was a man. And one day he caught a bear. It was a very fine bear, so he thought he would give it to the King.

So off they went, the man and the bear, tramp, tramp, tramp, to see the King. They hadn't gone very far when they came to a little house. And because it was very dark and they were afraid it was going to snow – because it was winter-time and so cold – they were pleased to see the little house. They knocked at the door to ask if they could come in. They thought, you see, that perhaps they could sleep inside in a cosy bed, instead of outside in the snow. For it would be a long time yet before they got to the King.

A man answered the door. 'May we come and sleep in your house?' said the bear-man.

'Oh dear, no,' said the man who opened the door. His name was Halvor.

'But it's cold out here,' said the bear-man.

'I know,' said Halvor.

'So may we come in?' said the bear-man.

'Oh dear, no,' said Halvor.

'But it's dark, and it's starting to snow,' said the bear-man.

'I know,' said Halvor.

'So may we come in?'

'Oh dear, no.'

'Well,' said the bear-man, 'that's a funny way to talk. Don't you want to help us and be kind to us?'

'Oh, I would very much like to help you,' said Halvor. 'But you see, it's Christmas-time. And every Christmas-time an enormous crowd of trolls come tearing into our house. They bang about, and they break the dishes, and they throw things, and they scream and shout, and they chase us right out of the house! Every Christmas-time! Isn't it a shame for our poor children – they never have a proper Christmas because of those trolls!'

'Oh, is it just trolls that are bothering you?' said the bear-man. 'We don't care about trolls. Just let us in and we'll sleep on the floor.'

So in the end Halvor let the man and the bear come in. And the bear lay down, while the man sat by the fire. And Halvor and his wife and their three children started to get the Christmas dinner ready; but, do you know, they did it with such sad faces because they knew that the trolls were going to chase them out before they could eat any of it.

Well, the next day was Christmas Day and they put that lovely dinner on the table. And sure enough, down the chimney came the trolls! Through the window came the trolls! Out of the fireplace came the trolls! And they banged about, and they broke the dishes, and they threw things, and they screamed and shouted. Halvor and his wife and the three children got up and ran out of the kitchen and out of the house and into the shed in the garden, and they locked the door.

But the man and the bear just sat still and watched. My, oh my, those trolls were naughty. They put their feet on the table, and they put their tails on the table, and they threw milk about, and they squashed up the cakes with their dirty toes, and they licked the jelly with their long, long tongues. The littlest ones were the worst of all. They climbed up the curtains, and they got on the shelves, and they started to throw down all the jars of jam and jars of honey and jars of pickled onions, right off the shelves. Smash! Crash! Oh, there was a mess!

Well, at last one of the littlest, naughtiest trolls suddenly saw the bear lying there very quiet and good. And the little troll found a piece of sausage and stuck it on a fork, and waved it about under the bear's nose, and shouted, 'Pussy, pussy! Have a sausage!' Oh, he was wild, that little troll! He poked the bear's nose with the fork. And just when the bear snapped at the sausage, he pulled it away so that the bear couldn't get it.

Then the great white bear was very, very angry. He got up from the floor, and he opened his mouth wide, and he roared at the top of his voice like thunder, and he chased those trolls right out of the house, big ones and little ones, those with tails and those without.

'Good boy!' said the bear-man. '*Good* boy!' And he gave him a whole sausage to eat. And he ate it nicely, making hardly any mess at all.

Then the bear-man called out, 'You can come out, Halvor, you and your wife and your three children. The trolls have gone away. My bear chased them out.' So Halvor and his wife and his three children unlocked the wood-shed and came out and came back to the house. They swept up the mess, and they scrubbed the table, and they picked up all the broken bits and put them in the dustbin. Then they all sat down to eat everything the trolls had left – and luckily they had left quite a lot, and it was very nice indeed. Then they all went to bed.

Next day, the bear-man said to Halvor, 'Thank you for having us. Now we must go to see the King.' And away went the man and the bear, and Halvor never saw them again, so I expect they found the King.

Now when Christmas Eve came round again the next year, Halvor was out chopping wood in the forest. Suddenly he heard someone calling far away through the trees. 'Halvor! Halvor!'

'What is it?' shouted Halvor.

'Have you still got your big white pussy-cat with you?'

'Yes, I have!' shouted Halvor. 'She's lying in front of the fire at home this minute. And she's got seven kittens now, and each of them is bigger and fiercer than she is herself. Now! What do you say to that?'

'Then, we'll never, never come to see you again!' shouted all the trolls.

15

And do you know, they never did, never. And now Halvor and his wife and his three children can always eat up their Christmas dinner just the same as everyone else.

ALF PRØYSEN

FATHER CHRISTMAS
AND THE CARPENTER

Translated by Marianne Helweg

There was once a carpenter called Anderson. He was a good father and he had a lot of children.

One Christmas Eve, while his wife and children were decorating the Christmas tree, Anderson crept out to his wood-shed. He had a surprise for them all; he was going to dress up as Father Christmas, load a sack of presents on to his sledge and go and knock on the front door. But as he pulled the loaded sledge out of the wood-shed, he slipped and fell across the sack of presents. This set the sledge moving, because the ground sloped from the sledge down to the road, and Anderson had no time to shout 'Way there!' before he crashed into another sledge which was coming down the road.

'I'm very sorry,' said Anderson.

'Don't mention it; I couldn't stop myself,' said the other man. Like Anderson, he was dressed in Father Christmas clothes and had a sack on his sledge.

'We seem to have the same idea,' said Anderson. 'I see you're all dressed up like me.' He laughed and shook the other man by the hand. 'My name is Anderson.'

'Glad to meet you,' said the other. 'I'm Father Christmas.'

17

'Ha, ha!' laughed Anderson. 'You will have your little joke, and quite right too on Christmas Eve.'

'That's what I thought,' said the other man, 'and if you will agree we can change places tonight, and that will be a better joke still; I'll take the presents along to your children if you'll go and visit mine. But you must take off that costume.'

Anderson looked a bit puzzled. 'What am I to dress up in, then?'

'You don't need to dress up at all,' said the other. 'My children see Father Christmas all the year round, but they've never seen a real carpenter. I told them last Christmas that if they were good this year I'd try to get a carpenter to come and see them while I went round with presents for human children.'

'So he really is Father Christmas,' thought Anderson to himself. Out loud he said, 'All right, if you really want me to,

I will. The only thing is, I haven't any presents for your children.'

'Presents?' said Father Christmas. 'Aren't you a carpenter?'

'Yes, of course.'

'Well, then, all you have to do is to take along a few pieces of wood, and some nails. You have a knife, I suppose?' Anderson said he had and went to look for the things in his workshop.

'Just follow my footsteps in the snow; they'll lead you to my house in the forest,' said Father Christmas. 'Then I'll take your sack and sledge and go and knock on your door.'

'Righto!' said the carpenter.

Then Father Christmas went to knock on Anderson's door, and the carpenter trudged through the snow in Father Christmas's footsteps. They led him into the forest, past two pine trees, a large boulder and a tree stump. There peeping out from behind the stump were three little faces with red caps on.

'He's here! He's here!' shouted the Christmas children as they scampered in front of him to a fallen tree, lying with its roots in the air. When Anderson followed them round to the other side of the roots he found Mother Christmas standing there waiting for him.

'Here he is, Mum! He's the carpenter Dad promised us! Look at him! isn't he tall!' The children were all shouting at once.

'Now, now, children,' said Mother Christmas. 'Anybody would think you'd never seen a human being before.'

'We've never seen a proper carpenter before!' shouted the children. 'Come on in, Mr Carpenter!'

Pulling a branch aside, Mother Christmas led the way into the house. Anderson had to bend his long back double and crawl on his hands and knees. But once in, he found he could straighten up. The room had a mud floor, but it was very cosy, with tree stumps for chairs, and beds made of moss with covers of plaited grass. In the smallest bed lay the Christmas baby and in the far corner sat a very old Grandfather Christmas, his red cap nodding up and down.

'Have you got a knife? Did you bring some wood and some nails?' The children pulled at Anderson's sleeve and wanted to know everything at once.

'Now, children,' said Mother Christmas, 'let the carpenter sit down before you start pestering him.'

'Has anyone come to see me?' croaked old Grandfather Christmas.

Mother Christmas shouted in his ear. 'It's Anderson, the carpenter!' She explained that Grandfather was so old he never went out any more. 'He'd be pleased if you would come over and shake hands with him.'

So Anderson took the old man's hand, which was as hard as a piece of bark.

'Come and sit here, Mr Carpenter!' called the children.

The eldest one spoke first. 'Do you know what I want you to make for me? A toboggan. Can you do that – a little one, I mean?'

'I'll try,' said Anderson, and it didn't take long before he had a smart toboggan just ready to fly over the snow.

'Now it's my turn,' said the little girl, who had pigtails sticking straight out from her head. 'I want a doll's bed.'

'Have you any dolls?' asked Anderson.

'No, but I borrow the field-mice sometimes, and I can play with baby squirrels as much as I like. They love being dolls. Please make me a doll's bed.'

So the carpenter made her a doll's bed. Then he asked the smaller boy what he would like. But he was very shy and could only whisper, 'Don't know.'

''Course he knows!' said his sister. 'He said it just before you came. Go on, tell the carpenter.'

'A top,' whispered the little boy.

'That's easy,' said the carpenter, and in no time at all he had made a top.

'And now you must make something for Mum!' said the children. Mother Christmas had been watching, but all the time she held something behind her back.

'Shush, children, don't keep bothering the carpenter,' she said.

'That's all right,' said Anderson. 'What would you like me to make?'

Mother Christmas brought out the thing she was holding; it was a wooden ladle, very worn, with a crack in it.

'Could you mend this for me, d'you think?' she asked.

'Hm, hm!' said Anderson, scratching his head with his carpenter's pencil. 'I think I'd better make you a new one.'

And he quickly cut a new ladle for Mother Christmas. Then he found a long twisted root with a crook at one end and started stripping it with his knife. But although the children asked him and asked him he wouldn't tell them what it was going to be. When it was finished he held it up; it was a very distinguished-looking walking stick.

'Here you are, Grandpa!' he shouted to the old man, and handed him the stick. Then he gathered up all the chips and made a wonderful little bird with wings outspread to hang over the baby's cot.

'How pretty!' exclaimed Mother Christmas and all the children. 'Thank the carpenter nicely now. We'll certainly never forget this Christmas Eve, will we?'

'Thank you, Mr Carpenter, thank you very much!' shouted the children.

Grandfather Christmas himself came stumping across the room leaning on his new stick. 'It's grand!' he said. 'It's just grand!'

There was the sound of feet stamping the snow off outside

the door, and Anderson knew it was time for him to go. He said good-bye all round and wished them a Happy Christmas. Then he crawled through the narrow opening under the fallen tree. Father Christmas was waiting for him. He had the sledge and the empty sack with him.

'Thank you for your help, Anderson,' he said. 'What did the youngsters say when they saw you?'

'Oh, they seemed very pleased. Now they're just waiting for you to come home and see their new toys. How did you get on at my house? Was little Peter frightened of you?'

'Not a bit,' said Father Christmas. 'He thought it was you. "Sit on Dadda's knee," he kept saying.'

'Well, I must go back to them,' said Anderson, and said good-bye to Father Christmas.

When he got home, the first thing he said to the children was, 'Can I see the presents you got from Father Christmas?'

But the children laughed. 'Silly! You've seen them already – when you were Father Christmas; you unpacked them all for us!'

'What would you say if I told you I have been with Father Christmas's family all this time?'

But the children laughed again. 'You wouldn't say anything so silly!' they said, and they didn't believe him. So the carpenter came to me and asked me to write down the story, which I did.

THE FAIRY SHIP

Little Tom was the son of a sailor. He lived in a small white-washed cottage in Cornwall, on the rocky cliffs looking over the sea. From his bedroom window he could watch the great waves with their curling plumes of white foam, and count the sea-gulls as they circled in the blue sky. The water went right away to the dim horizon, and sometimes Tom could see the smoke from ships like a dark flag in the distance. Then he ran to get his spy-glass, to get a better view.

Tom's father was somewhere out on that great stretch of ocean, and all Tom's thoughts were there, following him, wishing for him to come home. Every day he ran down the narrow path to the small rocky bay, and sat there waiting for the ship to return. It was no use to tell him that a ship could not enter the tiny cove with its sharp needles of rocks and dangerous crags. Tom was certain that he would see his sailor father step out to the strip of sand if he kept watch. It seemed the proper way to come home.

December brought wild winds that swept the coast. Little Tom was kept indoors, for the gales would have blown him away like a gull's feather if he had gone to the rocky pathway. He was deeply disappointed that he couldn't keep watch in his favourite place. A letter had come, saying that his father was on his way home and any time he might arrive. Tom feared he wouldn't be there to see him, and he stood by the window for hours watching the sky and the wild tossing sea.

'What shall I have for Christmas, Mother?' he asked one day. 'Will Father Christmas remember to bring me something?'

'Perhaps he will, if our ship comes home in time,' smiled his mother, and then she sighed and looked out at the wintry scene.

'Will he come in a sleigh with eight reindeer pulling it?' persisted Tom.

'Maybe he will,' said his mother, but she wasn't thinking what she was saying. Tom knew at once, and he pulled at her skirt.

'Mother! I don't think so. I don't think he will,' he said.

'Will what, Tom? What are you talking about?'

'Father Christmas won't come in a sleigh, because there isn't any snow here. Besides, it is too rocky, and the reindeer would slip. I think he'll come in a ship, a grand ship with blue sails and a gold mast.'

Little Tom took a deep breath and his eyes shone.

'Don't you think so, Mother? Blue sails, or maybe red ones. Satin like our parlour cushion. My father will come back with him. He'll come in a ship full of presents, and Father Christmas will give him some for me.'

Tom's mother suddenly laughed aloud.

'Of course he will, little Tom. Father Christmas comes in a sleigh drawn by a team of reindeer to the children of towns and villages, but to the children of the sea he sails in a ship with all the presents tucked away in the hold.'

She took her little son up in her arms and kissed him, but he struggled away and went back to the window.

'I'm going to be a sailor soon,' he announced proudly. 'Soon I shall be big enough, and then I shall go over the sea.'

He looked out at the stormy sea where his father was sailing, every day coming nearer home, and on that wild water he saw only mist and spray, and the cruel waves dashing over the jagged splinters of rock.

Christmas morning came, and it was a day of surprising sunshine and calm. The seas must have known it was Christmas and they kept peace and goodwill. They danced into the cove in sparkling waves, and fluttered their flags of white foam, and tossed their treasures of seaweed and shells on the narrow beach.

Tom awoke early, and looked in his stocking on the bed-post. There was nothing in it at all! He wasn't surprised. Land children had their presents dropped down the chimney, but he, a sailor's son, had to wait for the ship. The stormy weather had kept the Christmas ship at sea, but now she was bound to come.

His mother's face was happy and excited, as if she had a secret. Her eyes shone with joy, and she seemed to dance round the room in excitement, but she said nothing.

Tom ate his breakfast quietly – a bantam egg and some honey for a special treat. Then he ran outside, to the gate, and down the slippery grass path which led to the sea.

'Where are you going, Tom?' called his mother. 'You wait here, and you'll see something.'

'No, Mother. I'm going to look for the ship, the little Christmas ship,' he answered, and away he trotted, so his mother turned to the house, and made her own preparations for the man she loved. The tide was out and it was safe now the winds had dropped.

She looked through the window, and she could see the little boy sitting on a rock on the sand, staring away at the sea. His gold hair was blown back, his blue jersey was wrinkled about his stout little body. The gulls swooped round him as he tossed scraps of bread to feed them. Jackdaws came whirling from the cliffs and a raven croaked hoarsely from its perch on a rocky peak.

The water was deep blue, like the sky, and purple shadows hovered over it, as the waves gently rocked the cormorants fishing there. The little boy leaned back in his sheltered spot, and the sound of the water made him drowsy. The sweet air lulled him and his head began to droop.

Then he saw a sight so beautiful he had to rub his eyes to get the sleep out of them. The wintry sun made a pathway on the water, flickering with points of light on the crests of the waves, and down this golden lane came a tiny ship that seemed no larger than a toy. She moved swiftly through the water, making for the cove, and Tom cried out with joy and clapped his hands as she approached.

The wind filled the blue satin sails, and the sunbeams caught the mast of gold. On deck was a company of sailors dressed in white, and they were making music of some kind, for shrill squeaks and whistles and pipings came through the air. Tom leaned forward to watch them, and as the ship came nearer he could see that the little sailors were playing flutes, tootling a hornpipe, then whistling a carol.

He stared very hard at their pointed faces, and little pink ears. They were not sailor-men at all, but a crew of white mice! There were four-and-twenty of them – yes, twenty-four white mice with gold rings round their snowy necks, and gold rings in their ears!

The little ship sailed into the cove, through the barriers of sharp rocks, and the white mice hurried backward and forward, hauling at the silken ropes, casting the gold anchor, crying with high voices as the ship came to port close to the rock where Tom sat waiting and watching.

Out came the Captain – and would you believe it? He was a Duck, with a cocked hat like Nelson's, and a blue jacket trimmed with gold braid. Tom knew at once he was Captain Duck because under his wing he carried a brass telescope, and by his side was a tiny sword.

He stepped boldly down the gangway and waddled to the eager little boy.

'Quack! Quack!' said the Captain, saluting Tom, and Tom of course stood up and saluted back.

'The ship's cargo is ready, sir,' said the Duck. 'We have sailed across the sea to wish you a merry Christmas. You will find everything in order, sir. My men will bring the merchandise ashore, and here is the Bill of Lading.'

The Duck held out a piece of seaweed, and Tom took it. 'Thank you, Captain Duck,' said he. 'I'm not a very good reader yet, but I can count up to twenty-four.'

'Quack! Quack!' cried the Duck, saluting again. 'Quick! Quick!' he said, turning to the ship, and the four-and-twenty white mice scurried down to the cabin and dived into the hold.

Then up on deck they came, staggering under their burdens, dragging small bales of provisions, little oaken casks, baskets, sacks and hampers. They raced down the ship's ladders, and clambered over the sides, and swarmed down the gangway. They brought their packages ashore and laid them on the smooth sand near Tom's feet.

There were almonds and raisins, bursting from silken sacks. There were sugar-plums and goodies, pouring out of wicker baskets. There was a host of tiny toys, drums and marbles, tops and balls, pearly shells, and a flying kite, a singing bird and a musical-box.

When the last toy had been safely carried from the ship the white mice scampered back. They weighed anchor, singing 'Yo-heave-ho!' and they ran up the rigging. The Captain cried 'Quack! Quack!' and he stood on the ship's bridge. Before Tom could say 'Thank you,' the little golden ship began to sail away, with flags flying, and the blue satin sails tugging at the silken cords. The four-and-twenty white mice waved their sailor hats to Tom, and the Captain looked at him through his spy-glass.

Away went the ship, swift as the wind, a glittering speck on the waves. Away she went towards the far horizon along that bright path that the sun makes when it shines on water.

Tom waited till he could see her no more, and then he stooped over his presents. He tasted the almonds and raisins, he sucked the goodies, he beat the drum, and tinkled the musical-box and the iron triangle. He flew the kite, and tossed the balls in the air, and listened to the song of the singing-bird. He was so busy playing that he did not hear soft footsteps behind him.

Suddenly he was lifted up in a pair of strong arms and pressed against a thick blue coat, and two bright eyes were smiling at him.

'Well, Thomas, my son! Here I am! You didn't expect me, now did you? A Happy Christmas, Tom, boy. I crept down

soft as a snail, and you never heard a tinkle of me, did you?'

'Oh, Father!' Tom flung his arms round his father's neck and kissed him many times. 'Oh, Father! I knew you were coming. Look! They've been, they came just before you, in the ship.'

'Who, Tom? Who's been? I caught you fast asleep. Come along home and see what Father Christmas has brought you. He came along o' me, in my ship, you know. He gave me some presents for you.'

'He's been here already, just now, in a little gold ship, Father,' cried Tom, stammering with excitement. 'He's just sailed away. He was a Duck, Captain Duck, and there were four-and-twenty white mice with him. He left me all these toys. Lots of toys and things.'

Tom struggled to the ground, and pointed to the sand, but where the treasure of the fairy ship had been stored there was only a heap of pretty shells and seaweed and striped pebbles.

'They's all gone,' he cried, choking back a sob, but his father laughed and carried him off, pick-a-back, up the narrow footpath to the cottage.

'You've been dreaming, my son,' said he. 'Father Christmas came with me, and he's brought you a fine lot of toys, and I've got them at home for you.'

'Didn't dream,' insisted Tom. 'I saw them all.'

On the table in the kitchen lay such a medley of presents that Tom opened his eyes wider than ever. There were almonds and raisins, and goodies in little coloured sacks, and a musical-box with a picture of a ship on its round lid. There was a drum with scarlet edges, and a book, and a pearly shell from a far island, and a kite of thin paper from China, and a love-bird in a cage. Best of all there was a little model of his father's ship, which his father had carved for him.

'Why, these are like the toys from the fairy ship,' cried Tom. 'Those were very little ones, like fairy toys, and these are big ones, real ones.'

'Then it must have been a dream-ship,' said his mother. 'You must tell us all about it.'

So little Tom told the tale of the ship with blue satin sails and gold mast, and he told of the four-and-twenty white mice with gold rings round their necks, and the Captain Duck, who said 'Quack! Quack!' His father sat listening, as the words came tumbling from the excited little boy.

When Tom had finished, the sailor said, 'I'll sing you a song of that fairy ship, our Tom. Then you'll never forget what you saw.'

He waited a moment, gazing into the great fire on the hearth, and then he stood up and sang this song to his son and to his wife.

> There was a ship a-sailing,
> A-sailing on the sea.
> And it was deeply laden,
> With pretty things for me.
>
> There were raisins in the cabin,
> And almonds in the hold,
> The sails were made of satin,
> And the mast it was of gold.
>
> The four-and-twenty sailors
> That stood between the decks
> Were four-and-twenty white mice
> With rings about their necks.

33

The Fairy Ship

The Captain was a Duck, a Duck,
With a jacket on his back,
And when this fairy ship set sail,
The Captain he said 'Quack.'

'Oh, sing it again,' cried Tom, clapping his hands, and his father sang once more the song that later became a nursery rhyme.

It was such a lovely song that Tom hummed it all that happy Christmas Day, and it just fitted into the tune on his musical-box. He sang it to his children when they were little, long years later, and you can sing it too if you like!

IVAN GANTSCHEV

THE CHRISTMAS TRAIN

Translated by Stephen Corrin

Many years ago in a little railway station in Switzerland there lived a signalman named Wassil and his small daughter, Malina.

The railway track ran through many tunnels and was hemmed in by steep hills. It was part of Wassil's job to keep an eye on those dangerous stretches of the line.

One afternoon, the day before Christmas Eve, Wassil was checking the track while Malina was busy decorating the Christmas tree with the little stars she had made herself. She was eagerly looking forward to the present her father had promised to bring her.

Suddenly she heard a frightening rumble; it sounded like thunder. Her dog, Belo, began to bark and scratch at the door. 'It's the sound of falling rocks,' cried Malina, and she rushed outside, frightened out of her wits. Indeed, there, right in the middle of the track, lay an enormous boulder. Malina felt quite helpless. What on earth was she to do? 'The express will be here in half an hour. What would Daddy do? I must warn the engine-driver!' All sorts of thoughts flashed through her mind as she ran back indoors.

'Light a fire four hundred metres ahead of the spot where the accident happens and swing a lamp' – that's what her father had always told her to do if an emergency like this occurred.

Without further ado she picked up the Christmas tree, not bothering about the decorations, and snatched the big railwayman's lamp off its hook. Then she ran as fast as her legs

could carry her. There was barely a quarter of an hour left. By the light of the lamp she stumbled panting through a tunnel, then out again, hurrying between the rails till she got to a second tunnel. She could now hear the sound of the approaching train.

Hastily, with trembling hands, she set fire to the Christmas tree with the matches which she luckily hadn't forgotten to bring with her. Just at that very moment the express came thundering furiously from out of the black hole of the tunnel. The engine-driver shrank back with terror at the sight before his eyes. What he saw was a bright fire and a small child swinging a large red lamp. Immediately he slammed down the emergency brake and shut off the steam-regulator. The whistle shrieked. The great train juddered and came grinding and gasping to a gradual halt.

In the luxury restaurant-car everything flew wildly up and down again in tremendous confusion. The fish landed in the soup, the cream cakes went flying into the passengers' faces,

and the tablecloths wrapped themselves round the waiters. What a how-d'you-do!

Huffing and puffing, the giant locomotive had stopped just in front of Malina. Engine-driver and guard jumped out and rushed up to the little girl. The driver recognized her at once. 'It's Malina!' he exclaimed. 'What happened?'

'Down there, right in front of this next tunnel, a huge lump of rock has fallen down. I had to stop your train,' explained Malina breathlessly to the two startled men.

Meantime the news of the rock fall had travelled like wildfire through the train and soon everybody knew that little Malina had saved their lives.

'The child must be half frozen,' someone said. They took Malina by the hand and led her into the cosy warm dining-car.

A lot of mysterious whispering seemed to be going on among the passengers. Suddenly Malina found herself showered with presents. And then – her father appeared in the doorway! Cradled in his arms was a tiny lambkin – snow-white with black spots behind his ears. She ran up to him. This, she knew for sure, was her Christmas present.

'Come on, Dad,' Malina said, all excited, 'let's go home. Belo must be waiting for us.'

To show how grateful he was the engine-driver gave them a Christmas tree which he had freshly dug up from the station siding. So now they could celebrate Christmas properly after all.

And where, you may ask, did I hear this story? It's quite simple. Once *I* spent Christmas in that little railway station – with *my aunt* Malina and *my grandfather*, the signalman, Wassil.

PAUL BIEGEL

FATHER CHRISTMAS'S CLOTHES

Translated by Patricia Crampton

Joanna's cheeks were bright red with excitement. 'Listen!' she called, 'listen to this!' She rushed across the playground. 'He's coming to stay with us. In our house!'

'Huh?' asked Sylvia. 'Stay? Who?'

'Oh,' cried Joanna, 'Father Christmas, of course.'

'Father Christmas?'

Now all the children were crowding round her. 'Did you hear that? Father Christmas is coming to stay with Joanna.'

'Ha ha! He can't. Father Christmas never stays with anyone.' That was Billy.

'He must sleep somewhere, mustn't he?' That was Maria.

'But not in people's houses!'

'No. Where, then?'

'Father Christmas doesn't sleep. He rides over the roofs at night.'

'Yes, well then he must sleep in the daytime.'

'But not at Joanna's.'

'Yes!' cried Joanna. 'At our house. He's coming to stay with us. I saw it myself.'

'Saw what? Father Christmas?'

'No,' said Joanna, 'his clothes.' And she went on: 'The bell rang and there was a man at the door. He had a big box. And Mummy said: "Put it in the spare room." But she wouldn't tell me what was inside. So I went to have a look, when she wasn't watching. The box wasn't shut and Father Christmas's clothes were inside it. I saw them.'

The children stared, open-mouthed. But Billy said: 'I don't believe it.'

'Well,' said Joanna, 'you ask my Mum then.'

And they did. When school came out and Joanna's mother was standing at the gate waiting to pick up Joanna, all the children ran up to her.

'Mrs Green, Mrs Green, is it true, what Joanna says? That Father Christmas is coming to stay with you?'

Joanna's mother gave them an odd look. 'How did you get that idea?' she asked.

'Ha ha! Joanna said that Father Christmas's box of clothes was brought to your house.'

'Oh,' said Joanna's mother. Her cheeks turned a little red, as well. 'Yes, that is true. I didn't know you had seen that, Joanna.'

41

Oh dear! Joanna's face was fiery red.

'Oh well,' said her mother. 'What you said about the box is true, but as to Father Christmas coming to stay with us . . . I don't know for sure.'

'Oh?' cried Maria, 'how funny. Then why would he have his clothes brought to your house?'

'Uhum,' said Joanna's mother. She scratched her neck thoughtfully. 'I think he must be coming, just for a day or two.'

Then she took Joanna's hand and began to walk her quickly home.

The other children could see even from a distance that Joanna was getting into trouble – because she had given the secret away of course.

That night Joanna simply could not sleep. It's Christmas Eve the day after tomorrow, she thought. Father Christmas must have been travelling for a long time already and he will soon be here. But her mother had said that he would be much too busy to see Joanna.

'Father Christmas will only come home to sleep very late at night and he will have to be on his way again very early in the morning,' her mother said.

I shall have to be awake earlier still, thought Joanna. And I shall creep very quietly to the spare room. In her mind she could see Father Christmas lying in bed with his beard over the sheet. In *her* house. Would he snore?

But it was already late when Joanna woke up and when she looked, the spare room bed was quite smooth. The covers were all straight. Could Father Christmas have made the bed up himself before he left?

'That must be it,' said Sylvia, when Joanna told her about it. But Billy and the others did not believe it.

'He wasn't in your house at all,' they said. 'And he won't be coming, either.'

Joanna was very upset and that evening in bed she pressed her face hard into the pillows to stop the tears, until she suddenly heard movements in the spare room. With a leap Joanna was out of bed. Could it be . . . She crept into the passage, listened at the spare room door and opened it very quietly.

She got a dreadful fright: there was Father Christmas! Father Christmas himself, in his red coat and with his red hood on his head. He was standing in front of the looking glass, combing his beard.

Joanna's mouth fell open. 'Father –' she was about to gasp, but suddenly her arm was jerked, she was pulled back into the passage and the door was closed. It was her mother.

'Oh Joanna, you're not supposed to look. I mean: you

43

mustn't disturb Father Christmas. You must stay in bed and sleep.'

'Yes, but Mummy . . .'

It was no good. Joanna was tucked in again and soon afterwards she heard Father Christmas going out. Bang went the front door.

But I *did* see him, thought Joanna. I know he's true now and I know he's really staying with us.

'Ha, ha,' cried Billy next morning. 'I don't believe it. You're making it up.'

'I'm not.'

'You are.'

'I'm not.'

None of the children believed it except Sylvia, and of course she was Joanna's best friend. 'Do you know what?' said Sylvia. 'We'll come and pick you up to play tomorrow morning. It's Christmas Eve tomorrow and Father Christmas is sure to be there. He'll be having breakfast with you and we'll be able to see him for ourselves.'

Sylvia always had good ideas.

But Mummy looked thoughtful. 'I don't know if Father Christmas . . .' she began hesitantly, but suddenly Daddy said:

'I think he would. He'll need a good breakfast before he starts work, so he won't be leaving too early.'

Joanna was so excited that it took her a long time to get to sleep that night and her mother had to call her three times next morning. 'Father Christmas is having breakfast,' her mother called.

Am I dreaming? thought Joanna.

When she came down to the dining-room at last, Sylvia and

Maria and Billy and Ann and Jeremy and Martin and Freddie were there and . . . at the table, calmly spreading his toast, was Father Christmas. He actually had a little egg caught on his beard.

'How late you are, Joanna,' said Father Christmas. 'Come and sit down quickly.'

Joanna pinched herself to see if she was not dreaming after all. But Father Christmas was really there. He drank a cup of tea and ate another slice of toast and marmalade and all the children who had come, full of curiosity, to pick Joanna up, stood round watching him.

'Yes,' said Father Christmas. 'You wouldn't believe it, would you? But Joanna was right. She really had seen my box of clothes and where Father Christmas's clothes are, Father Christmas himself is not far away.'

RUTH SAWYER

SCHNITZLE, SCHNOTZLE
AND SCHNOOTZLE

The Tirol straddles the Alps and reaches one hand into Italy and another into Austria. There are more mountains in the Tirol than you can count and every Alp has its story.

Long ago, some say on the Brenner-Alp, some say on the Mitterwald-Alp, there lived the king of all the goblins of the Tirol, and his name was Laurin. King Laurin. His kingdom was under the earth, and all the gold and silver of the mountains he owned. He had a daughter, very young and very lovely, not at all like her father, who had a bulbous nose, big ears and a squat figure, and looked as old as the mountains. She loved flowers and was sad that none grew inside her father's kingdom.

'I want a garden of roses – red roses, pink roses, blush roses, flame roses, shell roses, roses like the sunrise and the sunset.' This she said one day to her father. And the king laughed and said she should have just such a garden. They would roof it with crystal, so that the sun would pour into the depths of the kingdom and make the roses grow lovely and fragrant. The garden was planted and every rare and exquisite rose bloomed in it. And so much colour they spread upwards on the

46

mountains around that the snow caught it and the *mortals* living in the valley pointed at it with wonder. 'What is it that makes our Alps so rosy, so glowing?' they asked. And they spoke of it ever after as the alpen-glow.

I have told you this that you might know what kind of goblin King Laurin was. He was merry, and he liked to play pranks and have fun. He liked to go abroad into the valleys where the *mortals* lived, or pop into a herdsman's hut halfway up the mountain. There were two men who said they had seen him – that small squat figure with a bulbous nose and big ears, gambolling with the goats on a summer day. And now I begin my story. It is an old one that Tirolese mothers like to tell to their children.

Long ago there lived in one of the valleys a very poor cobbler indeed. His wife had died and left him with three children, little boys all of them – Fritzl, Franzl, and Hansl. They lived in a hut so small there was only one room in it, and in that room was the cobbler's bench, a hearth for cooking, a big bed full of straw, and on the wall racks for a few dishes, and, of course, there was a table with a settle and some stools. They needed few dishes or pans, for there was never much to cook or eat. Sometimes the cobbler would mend the Sunday shoes of a farmer, and then there was good goat's milk to drink. Sometimes he would mend the holiday shoes of the baker, and then there was the good long crusty loaf of bread to eat. And sometimes he mended the shoes of the butcher, and then there was the good stew, cooked with meat in the pot, and noodles, leeks, and herbs. When the cobbler gathered the little boys around the table and they had said their grace, he would laugh and clap his hands and sometimes even dance. 'Ha-ha!' he would shout. 'Today we have the good . . . what?

Ah-h . . . today we eat . . . Schnitzle, Schnotzle, and Schnootzle!'

With that he would swing the kettle off the hook and fill every bowl brimming full, and Fritzl, Franzl, and Hansl would eat until they had had enough. Ach, those were the good days – the days of having Schnitzle, Schnotzle, and Schnootzle. Of course, the cobbler was making up nonsense and nothing else, but the stew tasted so much better because of the nonsense.

Now a year came, with every month following his brother on leaden feet. The little boys and the cobbler heard the month of March tramp out and April tramp in. They heard June tramp out and July tramp in. And every month marched heavier than his brother. And that was because war was among them again. War, with workers taking up their guns and leaving mothers and children to care for themselves as best they could; and there was scant to pay even a poor cobbler for mending shoes. The whole village shuffled to church with the soles flapping and the heels lopsided, and the eyelets and buttons and straps quite gone.

Summer – that was not so bad. But winter came and covered up the good earth, and gone were the roots, the berries, the sorrel, and the corn. The tramp of November going out and December coming in was very loud indeed. The little boys were quite sure that the two months shook the hut as they passed each other on the mountainside.

As Christmas grew near, the little boys began to wonder if there would be any feast for them, if there would be the good father dancing about the room and laughing, 'Ha-ha', and singing, 'Ho-ho', and saying: 'Now, this being Christmas Day we have the good . . .what?' And this time the little boys knew that they would never wait for their father to say it; they would shout themselves: 'We know – it is the good Schnitzle, Schnotzle, and Schnootzle!' Ach, how very long it was since their father had mended shoes for the butcher! Surely – surely – there would be need soon again, with Christmas so near.

At last came the Eve of Christmas. The little boys climbed along the beginnings of the Brenner-Alp, looking for faggots. The trees had shed so little that year; every branch was green and grew fast to its tree, so few twigs had snapped, so little was there of dead, dried bush to fill their arms.

Their father came in when they had a small fire started, blowing his whiskers free of icicles, slapping his arms about his big body, trying to put warmth back into it. 'Na-na, nobody will have a shoe mended today. I have asked everyone. Still, there is good news. The soldiers are marching into the village. The inn is full. They will have boots that need mending, those soldiers. You will see.' He pinched a cheek of each little boy; he winked at them and nodded his head. 'You shall see – tonight I will come home with . . .what?'

'Schnitzle, Schnotzle, and Schnootzle,' they shouted together, those three.

So happy they were they forgot there was nothing to eat for supper – not a crust, not a slice of cold porridge-pudding, not the smallest sup of goat's milk. 'Will the soldiers have money to pay you?' asked Fritzl, the oldest.

'Not the soldiers, perhaps, but the captains. There might even be a general. I will mend the boots of the soldiers for nothing, for after all what day is coming tomorrow? They fight for us, those soldiers; we mend for them, *ja*? But a general – he will have plenty of money.'

The boys stood about while their father put all his tools, all his pieces of leather into a rucksack; while he wound and wound and wound the woollen scarf about his neck, while he pulled the cap far down on his head. 'It will be a night to freeze

the ears off you,' he said. 'Now bolt the door after me, keep the fire burning with a little at a time; and climb into the straw bed and pull the quilt over you. And let no one in!'

He was gone. They bolted the door; they put a little on the fire; they climbed into the big bed, putting Hansl, the smallest, in the middle. They pulled up the quilt, such a thin quilt to keep out so much cold! Straight and still and close together they lay, looking up at the little spot of light the fire made on the ceiling, watching their breath go upwards in icy spurts. With the going of the sun the wind rose. First it whispered: it whispered of good fires in big chimneys; it whispered of the pines on the mountainsides; it whispered of the snow loosening and sliding over the glaciers. Then it began to blow: it blew hard, it blew quarrelsome, it blew cold and colder. And at last it roared. It roared its wintry breath through the cracks in the walls and under the door. And Fritzl, Franzl, and Hansl drew closer together and shivered.

'Whee . . . ooh . . . bang, bang! Whee . . . ooh . . . bang, bang!'

'Is it the wind or someone knocking?' asked Franzl.

'It is the wind,' said Fritzl.

'Whee . . . ooh . . . knock, knock!'

'Is it the wind or someone knocking?' asked Hansl.

'It is the wind and someone knocking!' said Fritzl.

He rolled out of the bed and went to the window. It looked out directly on the path to the door. 'Remember what our father said: do not open it,' said Franzl.

But Fritzl looked and looked. Close to the hut, beaten against it by the wind, stood a little man no bigger than Hansl. He was pounding on the door. Now they could hear him calling: 'Let me in! I tell you, let me in!'

'Oh don't, don't!' cried Hansl.

'I must,' said Fritzl. 'He looks very cold. The wind is tearing at him as a wolf tears at a young lamb', and with that he drew the bolt and into the hut skipped the oddest little man they had ever seen. He had a great peaked cap tied on to his head with deer-thongs. He had a round red face out of which stuck a bulbous nose, like a fat plum on a pudding. He had big

ears. And his teeth were chattering so hard they made the
stools to dance. He shook his fist at the three little boys. 'Ach,
kept me waiting. Wanted to keep all the good food, all the
good fire to yourselves? Na-na, that is no kind of hospitality.'

He looked over at the little bit of a fire on the hearth,
making hardly any heat in the hut. He looked at the empty
table, not a bowl set or a spoon beside it. He took up the big
pot, peered into it, turned it upside down to make sure
nothing was clinging to the bottom, set it down with a bang.
'So – you have already eaten it all. Greedy boys. But if you
have saved no feast for me, you can at least warm me.' With
that he climbed into the big straw-bed with Franzl and Hansl,
with his cap still tied under his chin. Fritzl tried to explain that
they had not been greedy, that there had never been any food,
not for days, to speak of. But he was too frightened of the little
man, of his eyes as sharp and blue as ice, of his mouth so
grumbling.

'Roll over, roll over,' the little man was shouting at the two in the bed. 'Can't you see I have no room? Roll over and give me half of the quilt.'

Fritzl saw that he was pushing his brothers out of the bed. 'Na-na,' he said, trying to make peace with their guest. 'They are little, those two. There is room for all if we but lie quiet.' And he started to climb into the bed himself, pulling gently at the quilt that there might be a corner for him.

But the little man bounced and rolled about, shouting: 'Give me room, give me more quilt. Can't you see I'm cold? I call this poor hospitality to bring a stranger inside your door, give him nothing to eat, and then grudge him bed and covering to keep him warm.' He dug his elbow into the side of skinny little Hansl.

'Ouch!' cried the boy.

Fritzl began to feel angry. 'Sir,' he said, 'sir, I pray you to be gentle with my little brother. And I am sorry there has been nothing to give you. But our father, the cobbler, has gone to mend shoes for the soldiers. When he returns we look for food. Truly, this is a night to feast and to share. So if you will but lie still until he comes I can promise you . . .'

The little man rolled over and stuck his elbow into Fritzl's ribs. 'Promise — promise. Na-na, what good is a promise? Come, get out of bed and give me your place.' He drew up his knees, put his feet in the middle of Fritzl's back and pushed with a great strength. The next moment the boy was spinning across the room. 'There you go,' roared the little man after him. 'If you must keep warm turn cartwheels, turn them fast.'

For a moment Fritzl stood sullenly by the small speck of fire. He felt bruised and very angry. He looked over at the bed. Sure enough, the greedy little man had rolled himself up in the quilt, leaving only a short corner of it for the two younger boys. He had taken more than half of the straw for himself, and was even then pushing and digging at Hansl. He saw Franzl raise himself up and take the place of his littlest brother, so that he should get the digs.

Brrr . . . it was cold! Before he knew it Fritzl was doing as he had been told, turning cartwheels around the room. He had rounded the table and was coming toward the bed when – plop! Plop – plop – plop! Things were falling out of his pockets every time his feet swung high over his head. Plop – plop – plop! The two younger boys were sitting up in bed. It was their cries of astonishment which brought Fritzl's feet back to the floor again, to stay. In a circle about the room, he had left behind him a golden trail of oranges. Such oranges – big as two fists! And sprinkled everywhere between were comfits wrapped in gold and silver paper. Fritzl stood and gaped at them.

'Here, you, get out and keep warm yourself!' shouted the little man as he dug Franzl in the ribs. 'Cartwheels for you, boy!' And the next minute Franzl was hurling in cartwheels about the room. Plop – plop – plop – things were dropping out of his pockets: Christmas buns, Christmas cookies covered with icing, with plums, with anise and caraway seeds.

The little man was now digging Hansl in the ribs. 'Lazy boy, greedy boy. Think you can have the bed to yourself now? Na-na, I'll have it! Out you go!' And he put his feet against the littlest boy's back and pushed him on to the floor. 'Cartwheels . . .' he began; but Fritzl, forgetting his amazement at what was happening, shouted: 'But, sir, he is too little. He cannot turn . . .'

'Hold him up in the corner, then. You keep warmer when your heels are higher than your head. Step lively there. Take a leg, each of you, and be quick about it.'

So angry did the little man seem, so fiery and determined, that Fritzl and Franzl hurried their little brother over to the chimney corner, stood him on his head and each held a leg. Donner and Blitzen! What happened then! Whack – whack – whickety-whack! Whack – whack – whickety-whack! Pelting the floor like hail against the roof came silver and gold pieces, all pouring out of Hansl's pockets.

Fritzl began to shout, Franzl began to dance. Hansl began to shout: 'Let me down, let me down!' When they did the three little boys danced around the pile, taking hands, singing 'Tra-la-la', and 'Fiddle-de-dee', and 'Ting-a-ling-a-ling', until their breath was gone and they could dance no longer.

They looked over at the bed and Fritzl was opening his mouth to say: 'Now, if you please, sir, we can offer you some Christmas cheer . . .' But the bed was empty, the quilt lay in a heap on the floor. The little man had gone.

The three little boys were gathering up the things on the floor – putting oranges into the big wooden bowl, buns and cookies on to the two platters, silver and gold pieces into this dish and that. And right in the midst of it in came their father, stamping, puffing in through the door. He had brought bread, he had brought milk, he had brought meat for the good stew – and noodles.

Such a wonder, such a clapping of hands, such a singing as they worked to get ready the Christmas feast! Fritzl began the story about their Christmas guest; Franzl told it mid-through; but little Hansl finished, making his brothers stand him in the corner again on his head to show just how it was that all the silver and gold had tumbled out of his pockets.

'Na-na,' said the cobbler, 'we are the lucky ones. I did not know it was true; always I thought it was a tale the grand-fathers told the children. The saying goes that King Laurin comes every year at the Christmas to one hut – one family – to play his tricks and share his treasure hoard.'

'He was a very ugly little man,' said Hansl. 'He dug us in our ribs and took all the bed for himself.'

'That was the king – that is the way he plays at being fierce. Say a special Christmas grace, then draw up the stools. Ah-h . . . what have we to eat?'

The little boys shouted the answer all together: 'Schnitzle – Schnotzle – Schnootzle!'

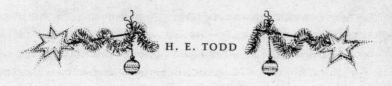

ANOTHER MINCE PIE

Christmas Day would never be the same without a Christmas tree, would it? Bobby Brewster doesn't think so, anyway. And there's another thing. He doesn't think that the Brewsters' tree would ever be the same without a fairy on top of it. One particular fairy. She has stood on the top of the tree every Christmas Day since Mrs Brewster was a little girl, and I'm not going to tell you how long ago that was.

For years Mrs Brewster has kept her in a drawer in the writing desk, packed in a little white box and wrapped in cotton wool. Then, late every Christmas Eve, there is a little ceremony when she is taken out of her box and put on top of the Christmas tree which always stands on the dining-room sideboard. On Boxing Day, back she goes into her snug white box for another year. That seems sad in a way, but she doesn't seem to mind because she's still smiling. Perhaps it's more comfortable in her box than balanced on top of a tree.

Now on last Christmas Day everything went very well as usual until dinner-time. The turkey was absolutely delicious, and everybody felt satisfied and rather sleepy when dinner was over. Then, as Bobby Brewster was clearing the clean things from the dinner table – a job he always does while the grown-ups wash up – a very funny thing happened. He heard the sound of crying.

'Who on earth can be crying on Christmas Day of all days?' he said to himself. At least, he thought he said it to himself, but he can't have done because a voice answered him. It did, really.

'*I'm* crying,' it said. 'And I'm *not* on earth, I'm on top of the Christmas tree.'

Bobby looked up, and there stood the poor little fairy crying her eyes out.

'Whatever's the matter?' he asked.

'I couldn't stand it any longer,' sobbed the fairy. 'Here I was all through your dinner-time smiling my head off, and there you were stuffing yourselves with turkey and Christmas pudding.'

'There's nothing wrong with that,' said Bobby. 'People always eat turkey and Christmas pudding for Christmas dinner. It's delicious, isn't it?'

'How should I know?' asked the fairy. 'All I've ever done is smell it and it certainly smells delicious. I've never tasted turkey and Christmas pudding in the whole of my life. It's not fair.' And she burst into tears again.

'Oh I say, I *am* sorry,' said Bobby. 'I had no idea you felt hungry. And I'm afraid the turkey and Christmas pudding have been cleared away.'

'What about a mince pie then?' suggested the fairy. 'There are some on the sideboard. May I have one of those, please?'

'Of course you may,' said Bobby. 'Where would you like it?'

'Put it on a small plate on the table and I will fly down and eat it,' said the fairy.

Bobby did as he was asked and the fairy opened her wings and landed on the dining-room table as lightly as a feather.

'What are you going to eat it with?' asked Bobby.

'Give me the little spoon from the salt-cellar,' replied the fairy, 'and I can use the star on the end of my wand for cutting it up.'

Well, it was a very large mince pie and she was a very small fairy, but Bobby gazed goggle-eyed as she tucked into it. In no time the mince pie was eaten right up.

'That was delicious,' said the fairy.

'I know,' agreed Bobby. 'My mother is always proud of her mince pies.'

'She has good reason to be,' said the fairy. 'Please give me another one, Bobby.'

So he did, and in no time that was eaten up as well.

'That was so nice that I do believe I could manage a third mince pie,' said the fairy, smacking her lips.

'Are you *quite* sure?' asked Bobby doubtfully.

'Absolutely positive,' said the fairy – and she was right too. It disappeared just as quickly as the others. Bobby wondered where on earth all the mince pie went to.

Then the fairy gave some instructions. 'Please leave another mince pie on my plate in case I feel hungry during the afternoon,' she said, 'and then I'll get on with my work.'

'Work?' repeated Bobby. 'I didn't know that anyone had to work on Christmas afternoon.'

'Oh dear me yes,' said the fairy. 'That's when I perform my most important task of the whole day.'

'Is it, indeed?' asked Bobby. 'And what is that?'

'Well,' continued the fairy, 'while you are playing with your presents on Christmas afternoon, what do you think the grown-ups are doing?'

'Going to sleep in the sitting-room of course,' Bobby answered promptly.

'Exactly,' agreed the fairy. 'And a disgusting sight they are, too. Slumped there in their chairs crammed full of turkey and Christmas pudding and with their mouths open. Some of them even snore.'

'I know,' agreed Bobby, 'especially my father. He makes a horrid noise.'

'What sort of a state do you expect them to be in when they wake up then?' asked the fairy.

'I'm sure I don't know,' said Bobby. 'I've never actually been there when they wake up. They always seem cheerful enough at tea-time, and on Christmas evening they're full of fun.'

'Thanks to me,' said the fairy. 'When grown-ups wake up in the afternoon after eating too much dinner they are usually very grumpy, and that would never do for Christmas evening, would it? That's where I come in. While they are still asleep I fly into the sitting-room, touch them gently on the head with my wand, and whisper, "May you be filled with the spirit of Christmas." And it always works. When they wake up, they are.'

'Well goodness me,' cried Bobby, 'so we have *you* to thank for all our jolly Christmas evenings.'

'Partly,' said the fairy modestly. 'Me and Father Christmas.'

'It's very kind of you,' said Bobby.

'That's all right,' said the fairy. 'I enjoy it. Now you run along and play with your new toys while I eat another mince pie.'

'*Another* one!' cried Bobby.

'Of course,' said the fairy. 'After that *I* will have a little nap before I fly into the sitting-room with my magic wand. I think I deserve it, don't you?'

'You certainly do,' Bobby assured her. 'Especially after all those mince pies. Be sure to wake up in time, won't you?'

'Don't worry,' said the fairy confidently. 'My magic *always* works.'

But for once she was wrong. Bobby had a lovely time playing with his toys, and then he began to wonder whether it was tea-time. He wasn't hungry, because no one ever is at tea-time on Christmas Day, but it had turned dark outside. He went into the sitting-room, and there sat his mother and father looking a picture of misery.

'I don't want any tea,' said Mrs Brewster. 'I've got a terrible headache. It feels as if there has been a load on top of my head for the whole afternoon.'

'I've got a terrible headache too,' complained Mr Brewster. 'And there's a scratch on my forehead. I must have knocked it on the side of my chair while I was alseep. No wonder my head aches.'

Bobby ran into the dining-room to tell the fairy. He was just going to say, 'I don't think much of your magic,' when he caught sight of her. She wasn't standing on top of the tree. She was sitting with her head in her hands on a broken silver ball at the bottom of the tree. Her crown was askew, her hair all over the place, one of her wings was bent, and there was no sign of the magic wand.

'Whatever's the matter?' gasped Bobby.

'Oh dear, oh dear,' moaned the fairy. 'It's all those mince pies. When I woke up I felt awful, and I had the greatest difficulty in flying into the sitting-room.'

'You didn't do much good when you *did* fly there,' complained Bobby. 'My mother says her head feels as if there had been a load on it for the whole afternoon.'

'There was,' said the fairy. 'It was me. I landed far too heavily on her head in the first place. Then I couldn't take off again and I had to sit down on her head for half an hour. And I was so flustered that I forgot to touch her with my magic wand and say, "May you be filled with the spirit of Christmas." So she isn't.'

'She certainly isn't,' agreed Bobby. 'But there's worse than that. Not only has my father got a headache too, but there's a nasty scratch on his forehead.'

'That's me too,' said the fairy. 'When I was hovering over him ready to land I dropped my magic wand. The sharp edge of the star hit him on the forehead, and then it bounced to the floor. I couldn't find it anywhere, and it wasn't the slightest use whispering "May you be filled with the spirit of Christmas" without it. So he isn't either.'

'Oh dear,' said Bobby. 'It's going to be an awful Christmas evening. Whatever can we do?'

'The first thing you must do,' said the fairy, 'is to go back into the sitting-room and find my magic wand. I'm useless without it.'

When Bobby returned to the sitting-room his mother was sticking a piece of plaster over the scratch on his father's head. Bobby knelt down on all fours and groped around his father's chair.

'Whatever are you doing, Bobby?' snapped his mother – and she didn't sound at all Christmassy.

'I'm just looking for something,' said Bobby mysteriously, and luckily before she asked him to explain himself he saw something glittering underneath the coal scuttle. It was the star on top of the fairy's wand. He picked the wand up quickly and hid it in his hand.

Then Bobby Brewster had an idea. 'If the magic wand works for the fairy,' he said to himself, 'it might even work for me.'

By that time his mother had finished sticking the plaster on his father's forehead, and they were both back sitting in their chairs looking thoroughly miserable. Bobby leant over his father and pretended to inspect the plaster. Then he gently touched him on top of the head with the star on the magic wand and whispered 'May you be filled with the spirit of Christmas.'

Mr Brewster didn't hear anything, but at once a smile spread over his face. 'Do you know,' he said. 'There must have been something magic about that plaster. My headache is suddenly much better.'

'I wish mine was,' moaned Mrs Brewster.

Bobby tiptoed over to the back of her chair and pretended to stroke her head. As he did so he touched her with the magic wand and whispered again, 'May you be filled with the spirit of Christmas.' And she was – straight away.

'Do you know,' she said. 'My headache is suddenly better too. I must go and get the tea.'

While she was in the kitchen Bobby returned to the dining-room. The poor fairy was still sitting on the broken silver ball with her head in her hands.

'Oh dear,' she cried. 'I've spoilt everything.'

'Don't worry,' said Bobby in a soothing voice. Then he had another idea – an even better one. 'If the magic wand works for me on Mother and Father,' he said to himself, 'it might even work for me on the fairy herself.'

This time he didn't try to hide anything because he didn't think that was necessary. What would be the point of hiding magic from a fairy? He touched the fairy gently on her crown with her own wand and said distinctly, 'May you be filled with the spirit of Christmas.'

The sweet smile returned to her face and her wing unbent itself. She sat up and tidied her hair with her hands and put the crown straight. Then she flew as lightly as a feather above the Christmas tree and made a perfect landing on the top.

Bobby sighed with relief. It was going to be a happy Christmas evening for everybody after all. And it was – the best Christmas evening he had ever spent.

When it was all over and Bobby was about to go to bed he thought he would go and say good-night to the Christmas tree fairy.

'Thank you very much for everything,' he said. 'We had a lovely evening.'

'Thank *you* very much for being so clever,' replied the fairy, and Bobby felt quite proud of himself.

'Before I go to bed,' he asked, 'is there anything else I can do for you?'

'Yes please,' said the fairy wistfully.

'What is it?' asked Bobby.

'I should like another mince pie,' said the fairy.

THE NAUGHTIEST STORY
OF ALL

This is such a very terrible story about my naughty little sister that I hardly know how to tell it to you. It is all about one Christmas-time.

Now, my naughty little sister was very pleased when Christmas began to draw near, because she liked all the excitement of the plum-puddings and the turkeys, and the crackers and the holly, and all the Christmassy-looking shops, but there was one very awful thing about her – she didn't like to think about Father Christmas at all – she said he was a horrid old man!

There – I knew you would be shocked at that. But she did. And she said she wouldn't put up her stocking for him.

My mother told my naughty little sister what a good old man Father Christmas was, and how he brought the toys along on Christmas Eve, but my naughty little sister said, 'I don't care. And I don't want that nasty old man coming to our house.'

Well now, that was bad enough, wasn't it? But the really dreadful thing happened later on.

This is the dreadful thing: one day, my school-teacher said that a Father Christmas Man would be coming to the school to

67

bring presents for all the children, and my teacher said that the Father Christmas Man would have toys for all our little brothers and sisters as well, if they cared to come along for them. She said there would be a real Christmas-tree with candles on it, and sweeties and cups of tea and biscuits for our mothers.

Wasn't that a nice thought? Well now, when I told my little sister about the Christmas-tree, she said, 'Oh, nice!'

And when I told her about the sweeties she said, 'Very, very nice!' But when I told her about the Father Christmas Man, she said, 'Don't want him, nasty old man.'

Still, my mother said, 'You can't go to the Christmas-tree without seeing him, so if you don't want to see him all that much, you will have to stay at home.'

But my naughty little sister did want to go, very much, so she said, 'I will go, and when the horrid Father Christmas Man comes in, I will close my eyes.'

So, we all went to the Christmas-tree together, my mother, and I, and my naughty little sister.

When we got to the school, my naughty little sister was very pleased to see all the pretty paperchains that we had made in school hanging all round the classrooms, and when she saw all the little lanterns, and the holly, and all the robin-redbreast drawings pinned on the blackboards she smiled and smiled. She was very smily at first.

All the mothers, and the little brothers and sisters who were too young for school, sat down in chairs and desks, and all the big school children acted a play for them.

My little sister was very excited to see all the children dressed up as fairies and robins and elves and Bo-peeps and things, and she clapped her hands very hard, like all the

grown-ups did, to show that she was enjoying herself. And she still smiled.

Then, when some of the teachers came round with bags of sweets, tied up in pretty coloured paper, my little sister smiled even more, and she sang too when all the children sang. She sang, 'Away in a manger', because she knew the words very well. When she didn't know the words of some of the singing, she 'la-la'd'.

After all the singing, the teachers put out the lights, and took away a big screen from a corner of the room, and there was the Christmas-tree, all lit up with candles and shining with silvery stuff, and little shiny coloured balls. There were lots of toys on the tree, and all the children cheered and clapped.

Then the teachers put the lights on again, and blew out the candles, so that we could all go and look at the tree. My little sister went too. She looked at the tree, and she looked at the toys, and she saw a specially nice doll with a blue dress on, and she said, 'For me.'

My mother said, 'You must wait and see what you are given.'

Then the teachers called out, 'Back to your seats, everyone, we have a visitor coming.' So all the children went back to their seats, and sat still and waited and listened.

And, as we waited and listened, we heard a tinkle-tinkle bell noise, and then the schoolroom door opened, and in walked the Father Christmas Man. My naughty little sister had forgotten all about him, so she hadn't time to close her eyes before he walked in. However, when she saw him, my little sister stopped smiling and began to be stubborn.

The Father Christmas Man was very nice. He said he hoped we were having a good time, and we all said, 'Yes,' except my naughty little sister – she didn't say a thing.

Then he said, 'Now, one at a time, children; and I will give each one of you a toy.'

So, first of all each schoolchild went up for a toy, and my naughty little sister still didn't shut her eyes because she wanted to see who was going to have the specially nice doll in the blue dress. But none of the schoolchildren had it.

Then Father Christmas began to call the little brothers and sisters up for presents, and, as he didn't know their names, he just said, 'Come along, sonny,' if it were a boy, and 'Come along, girlie,' if it were a girl. The Father Christmas Man let the little brothers and sisters choose their own toys off the tree.

When my naughty little sister saw this, she was so worried about the specially nice doll that she thought that she would just go up and get it.

She said, 'I don't like that horrid old beardy man, but I do like that nice doll.'

So, my naughty little sister got up without being asked to, and she went right out to the front where the Father Christmas Man was standing, and she said, 'That doll, please,' and pointed to the doll she wanted.

The Father Christmas Man laughed and all the teachers laughed, and the other mothers and the schoolchildren, and all the little brothers and sisters. My mother did not laugh because she was so shocked to see my naughty little sister going out without being asked to.

The Father Christmas Man took the specially nice doll off the tree, and he handed it to my naughty little sister and he

said, 'Well now, I hear you don't like me very much, but won't you shake hands?' and my naughty little sister said, 'No.' But she took the doll all the same.

The Father Christmas Man put out his nice old hand for her to shake and be friends, and do you know what that naughty bad girl did? She bit his hand. She really and truly did. Can you think of anything more dreadful and terrible? She bit Father Christmas's good old hand, and then she turned and ran and ran out of the school with all the children staring after her, and her doll held very tight in her arms.

The Father Christmas Man was very nice. He said it wasn't a hard bite, only a frightened one, and he made all the children sing songs together.

When my naughty little sister was brought back by my mother, she said she was very sorry, and the Father Christmas Man said, 'That's all right, old lady,' and because he was so smily and nice to her, my funny little sister went right up to him, and gave him a big 'sorry' kiss, which pleased him very much.

And she hung her stocking up after all, and that kind man remembered to fill it up for her.

My little sister kept the specially nice doll until she was

quite grown-up. She called it Rosy-Primrose, and although she was sometimes bad-tempered with it, she really loved it very much indeed.

RUTH SAWYER

THE VOYAGE
OF THE WEE RED CAP

It was the Eve of Saint Stephen, and Teig sat alone by his fire with naught in his cupboard but a pinch of tea and a bare mixture of meal, and a heart inside of him as soft and warm as the ice on the water-bucket outside the door. The turf was near burnt on the hearth – a handful of golden cinders left, just; and Teig took to counting them greedily on his fingers.

'There's one, two, three, an' four an' five,' he laughed. 'Faith, there be more bits o' real gold hid undther the loose clay in the corner.'

It was the truth; and it was the scraping and scrooching for the last piece that had left Teig's cupboard bare of a Christmas dinner.

'Gold is betther nor eatin' an' dthrinkin'. An' if ye have naught to give, there'll be naught asked of ye.' And he laughed again.

He was thinking of the neighbours, and the doles of food and piggins of milk that would pass over their thresholds that night to the vagabonds and paupers who were sure to come begging. And on the heels of that thought followed another: Who would be giving old Barney his dinner? Barney lived a stone's throw from Teig, alone in a wee tumbled-in cabin; and

74

for a score of years past Teig had stood on the doorstep every Christmas Eve and, making a hollow of his two hands, had called across the road:

'Hey, there, Barney, will ye come over for a sup?'

And Barney had reached for his crutches – there being but one leg to him – and had come.

'Faith,' said Teig, trying another laugh, 'Barney can fast for the once; 'twill be all the same in a month's time.' And he fell to thinking of the gold again.

A knock came at the door. Teig pulled himself down in his

chair where the shadow would cover him, and held his tongue.

'Teig, Teig!' It was the Widow O'Donnelly's voice. 'If ye are there, open your door. I have not got the pay for the spriggin' this month, an' the childher are needin' food.'

But Teig put the leash on his tongue, and never stirred till he heard the tramp of her feet going on to the next cabin. Then he saw to it that the door was tight barred. Another knock came, and it was a stranger's voice this time:

'The other cabins are filled; not one but has its hearth crowded; will ye take us in – the two of us? The wind bites mortal sharp, not a morsel o' food have we tasted this day. Masther, will ye take us in?'

But Teig sat on, a-holding his tongue; and the tramp of the strangers' feet passed down the road. Others took their place – small feet, running. It was the miller's wee Cassie, and she called out as she ran by:

'Old Barney's watchin' for ye. Ye'll not be forgettin' him, will ye, Teig?'

And then the child broke into a song, sweet and clear, as she passed down the road:

Hearken all ye, 'tis the Feast o' Saint Stephen,
Mind that ye keep it this holy even.
Open your door an' greet ye the stranger,
For ye mind that the wee Lord had naught but a manger.

Teig put his fingers deep in his ears. 'A million murdthering curses on them that won't let me be! Can't a man try to keep what is his without bein' pesthered by them that has only idled and wasted their days?'

And then the strange thing happened: hundreds and hundreds of wee lights began dancing outside the window, making the room bright; the hands of the clock began chasing each other round the dial; and the bolt of the door drew itself out. Slowly, without a creak or a cringe, the door opened, and in there trooped a crowd of the Good People. Their wee green cloaks were folded close about them, and each carried a rush candle.

Teig was filled with a great wonderment, entirely, when he saw the fairies, but when they saw him they laughed.

'We are takin' the loan o' your cabin this night, Teig,' said they. 'Ye are the only man hereabouts with an empty hearth an' we're needin' one.'

Without saying more, they bustled about the room making ready. They lengthened out the table and spread and set it; more of the Good People trooped in bringing stools and food and drink. The pipers came last, and they sat themselves around the chimney-piece a-blowing their chanters and trying the drones. The feasting began and the pipers played, and never had Teig seen such a sight in his life. Suddenly, a wee man sang out:

'Clip clap, clip clap, I wish I had my wee red cap!' And out of the air there tumbled the neatest cap Teig ever laid his two eyes on. The wee man clapped it on his head, crying: 'I wish I was in Spain!' and – whist – up the chimney he went, and away out of sight.

It happened just as I am telling it. Another wee man called for his cap, and away he went after the first. And then another and another, until the room was empty and Teig sat alone again.

'By my soul,' said Teig, 'I'd like to travel that way myself! It's a grand savin' of tickets an' baggage; an' ye get to a place before ye've had time to change your mind. Faith, there's no harm done if I thry it.'

So he sang the fairies' rhyme, and out of the air dropped a wee cap for him. For a moment the wonder had him, but the next he was clapping the hat on his head and crying:

'Spain!'

Then – whist – up the chimney he went after the fairies, and before he had time to let out his breath he was standing in the middle of Spain, and strangeness all about him.

He was in a great city. The doorways of the houses were hung with flowers and the air was warm and sweet with the smell of them. Torches burned along the streets, sweetmeat-sellers went about crying their wares, and on the steps of the cathedral crouched a crowd of beggars.

'What's the meanin' o' that?' asked Teig of one of the fairies.

'They are waiting for those that are hearing the Mass. When they come out, they give half of what they have to those that have nothing, so on this night of all the year there shall be no hunger and no cold.'

And then far down the street came the sound of a child's voice, singing:

> Hearken all ye, 'tis the Feast o' Saint Stephen,
> Mind that ye keep it this holy even.

'Curse it!' said Teig. 'Can a song fly afther ye?' And then he heard the fairies cry 'Holland!' and cried 'Holland!' too.

In one leap he was over France, and another over Belgium, and with the third he was standing by long ditches of frozen water, and over them glided hundreds upon hundreds of lads and maids. Outside each door stood a wee wooden shoe, empty. Teig saw scores of them as he looked down the ditch of a street.

'What is the meanin' o' those shoes?' he asked the fairies.

'Ye poor lad!' answered the wee man next to him. 'Are ye not knowing anything? This is the Gift Night of the year, when every man gives to his neighbour.'

A child came to the window of one of the houses, and in her hand was a lighted candle. She was singing as she put the light down close to the glass, and Teig caught the words:

Open your door an' greet ye the stranger,
For ye mind that the wee Lord had naught but a manger.

''Tis the devil's work!' cried Teig, and he set the red cap more firmly on his head. 'I'm for another country.'

I cannot be telling you a half of the adventures Teig had that night, nor half the sights he saw. But he passed by fields that held sheaves of grain for the birds and doorsteps that held bowls of porridge for the wee creatures. He saw lighted trees, sparkling and heavy with gifts; and he stood outside the churches and watched the crowds pass in, bearing gifts to the Holy Mother and Child.

At last the fairies straightened their caps and cried: 'Now for the great hall in the King of England's palace!'

Whist – and away they went, and Teig after them; and the first thing he knew he was in London, not an arm's length from the King's throne. It was a grander sight than he had seen in any other country. The hall was filled entirely with lords and ladies; and the great doors were open for the poor and the homeless to come in and warm themselves by the King's fire and feast from the King's table. And many a hungry soul did the King serve with his own hands.

Those that had anything to give gave it in return. It might be a bit of music played on a harp or a pipe, or it might be a dance or a song; but more often it was a wish, just, for good luck and safekeeping.

Teig was so taken up with the watching that he never heard the fairies when they wished themselves off; moreover, he never saw the wee girl that was fed and went laughing away. But he heard a bit of her song as she passed through the door:

> Feed ye the hungry an' rest ye the weary,
> This ye must do for the sake of Our Mary.

Then the anger had Teig. 'I'll stop your pestherin' tongue,

once an' for all time!' and, catching the cap from his head, he threw it after her.

No sooner was the cap gone than every soul in the hall saw him. The next moment they were about him, catching at his coat and crying:

'Where is he from, what does he here? Bring him before the King!' And Teig was dragged along by a hundred hands to the throne where the King sat.

'He was stealing food,' cried one.

'He was robbing the King's jewels,' cried another.

'He looks evil,' cried a third. 'Kill him!'

And in a moment all the voices took it up and the hall rang with: 'Aye, kill him, kill him!'

Teig's legs took to trembling, and fear put the leash on his tongue; but after a long silence he managed to whisper:

'I have done evil to no one – no one!'

'Maybe,' said the King; 'but have ye done good? Come, tell us, have ye given aught to anyone this night? If ye have, we will pardon ye.'

Not a word could Teig say. Fear tightened the leash, for he was knowing full well there was no good to him that night.

'Then ye must die,' said the King. 'Will ye try hanging or beheading?'

'Hanging, please, your Majesty,' said Teig.

The guards came rushing up and carried him off. But as he was crossing the threshold of the hall a thought sprang at him and held him, just.

'Your Majesty,' he called after him, 'will ye grant me a last request?'

'I will,' said the King.

'Thank ye. There's a wee red cap that I'm mortal fond of, and I lost it a while ago; if I could be hung with it on, I would hang a deal more comfortable.'

The cap was found and brought to Teig.

'Clip clap, clip clap, for my wee red cap, I wish I was home,' he sang.

Up and over the heads of the dumbfounded guard he flew – whist, and away out of sight. When he opened his eyes again, he was sitting close by his own hearth, with the fire burnt low. The hands of the clock were still, the bolt was fixed firm in the door. The fairies' lights were gone, and the only bright thing was the candle burning in old Barney's cabin across the road.

A running of feet sounded outside, and then a snatch of a song:

'Tis well that ye mind – ye who sit by the fire –
That the Lord He was born in a dark and cold byre.

'Wait ye, whoever ye are!' And Teig was away to the corner, digging fast at the loose clay, as a terrier digs at a bone. He filled his hands full of the shining gold, then hurried to the door, unbarring it.

The miller's wee Cassie stood there, peering at him out of the darkness.

'Take those to the Widow O'Donnelly, do ye hear? And take the rest to the store. Ye tell Jamie to bring up all that he has that is eatable an' dthrinkable; and to the neighbours ye say: "Teig's keepin' the feast this night." Hurry, away!'

Teig stopped a moment on the threshold until the tramp of her feet had died away; then he made a hollow of his two hands and called across the road:

'Hey, there, Barney, will ye come over for a sup?'

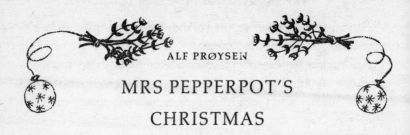

ALF PRØYSEN

MRS PEPPERPOT'S
CHRISTMAS

Translated by Marianne Helweg

There was once a little old woman who went to bed at night like everyone else, but sometimes in the morning she would wake up and find that she had *shrunk* to the size of a pepperpot. As it happens her name was Mrs Pepperpot.

This was one of those mornings, and Mrs Pepperpot climbed to the top of the bed-post and swung her legs while she wondered what to do.

'What a nuisance!' she said. 'Just when I wanted to go to the Christmas Market with Mr Pepperpot!'

She wanted to buy a sheaf of corn for the birds' Christmas dinner, and she wanted to get them a little bird-house where she could feed them every day. The other thing she wanted was a wreath of mistletoe to hang over the door, so that she could wish Mr Pepperpot a 'Happy Christmas' with a kiss. But Mr Pepperpot thought this was a silly idea.

'Quite unnecessary!' he said.

But Mrs Pepperpot was very clever at getting her own way; so even though she was now no bigger than a mouse, she soon worked out a plan. She heard her husband put his knapsack down on the floor in the kitchen and – quick as a flash – she slid down the bed-post, scuttled over the doorstep and climbed into one of the knapsack pockets.

Mr Pepperpot put the knapsack on his back and set off through the snow on his kick-sledge, while Mrs Pepperpot peeped out from the pocket.

'Look at all those nice cottages!' she said to herself. 'I bet every one of them has a sheaf of corn and a little house for the birds. *And* they'll have mistletoe over the door as well, no doubt. But you wait till I get home; I'll show them!'

At the market there were crowds of people both big and small; everyone was doing their Christmas shopping, and there was plenty to choose from! At one stall stood a farmer selling beautiful golden sheaves of corn. As her husband walked past the stall Mrs Pepperpot climbed out from the knapsack pocket and disappeared inside the biggest sheaf of all.

'Hullo, Mr Pepperpot,' said the farmer, 'how about some corn for the birds this Christmas?'

'Too dear!' answered Mr Pepperpot gruffly.

'Oh no, it's not!' squeaked the little voice of Mrs Pepperpot. 'If you don't buy this sheaf of corn I'll tell everyone you're married to the woman who *shrinks*!'

Now Mr Pepperpot hated people to know about his wife turning small, so when he saw her waving to him from the

biggest sheaf he said to the farmer: 'I've changed my mind; I'll have that one, please!'

But the farmer told him he would have to wait in the queue.

Only a little girl saw Mrs Pepperpot slip out of the corn and dash into a bird-house on Mr Andersen's stall. He was a carpenter and made all his bird-houses look just like real little houses with doors and windows for the birds to fly in and out. Of course Mrs Pepperpot chose the prettiest house; it even had curtains in the windows and from behind these she watched her husband buy the very best sheaf of corn and stuff it in his knapsack.

He thought his wife was safe inside and was just about to get on his kick-sledge and head for home, when he heard a little voice calling him from the next stall.

'Hullo, husband!' squeaked Mrs Pepperpot. 'Haven't you forgotten something? You were going to buy me a bird-house!'

Mr Pepperpot hurried over to the stall. He pointed to the house with the curtains and said: 'I want to buy that one, please!'

Mr Andersen was busy with his customers. 'You'll have to take your turn,'' he said.

So once more poor Mr Pepperpot had to stand patiently in a queue. He hoped that no one else would buy the house with his wife inside.

But she *wasn't* inside; she had run out of the back door, and now she was on her way to the next stall.

Here there was a pretty young lady selling holly and

mistletoe. Mrs Pepperpot had to climb up the post to reach the nicest wreath, and there she stayed hidden.

Soon Mr Pepperpot came by, carrying both the sheaf of corn and the little bird-house. The young lady gave him a dazzling smile and said:

'Oh, Mr Pepperpot, wouldn't you like to buy a wreath of mistletoe for your wife?'

'No thanks,' said Mr Pepperpot, 'I'm in a hurry.'

> 'Swing high! Swing low!
> I'm in the mistletoe!'

sang Mrs Pepperpot from her lofty perch.

When Mr Pepperpot caught sight of her his mouth fell open. 'Oh dear!' he groaned. 'This is too bad!'

With a shaking hand he paid the young lady the right money and lifted the wreath down himself, taking care that Mrs Pepperpot didn't slip out of his fingers. *This* time there would be no escape; he would take his wife straight home, whether she liked it or not.

But just as he was leaving, the young lady said: 'Oh sir, you're our one hundredth customer, so you get a free balloon!' and she handed him a red balloon.

Before anyone could say 'Jack Robinson' Mrs Pepperpot had grabbed the string and, while Mr Pepperpot was struggling with his purse, gloves and parcels, his tiny wife was soaring up into the sky.

Up she went over the market-place, and soon she was fluttering over the trees of the forest, followed by a crowd of crows and magpies and small birds of every sort.

'Here I come!' she shouted in bird-language. For, when Mrs Pepperpot was small she could talk with animals and birds.

A big crow cawed: 'Are you going to the moon with that balloon?'

'Not quite, I hope!' said Mrs Pepperpot, and she told them the whole story. The birds all squawked with glee when they

heard about the corn and the bird-house she had got for them.

'But first you just help *me*,' said Mrs Pepperpot. 'I want you all to hang on to this balloon string and guide me back to land on my own doorstep.'

So the birds clung to the string with their beaks and claws and, as they flew down to Mrs Pepperpot's house, the balloon looked like a kite with fancy bows tied to its tail.

When Mrs Pepperpot set foot on the ground she instantly grew to her normal size.

So she waved good-bye to the birds and went indoors to wait for Mr Pepperpot.

It was late in the evening before Mr Pepperpot came home, tired and miserable after searching everywhere for his lost wife. He put his knapsack down in the hall and carried the sheaf of corn and the bird-house outside. But when he came in again he noticed that the mistletoe had disappeared.

'Oh well,' he said sadly, 'what does it matter now that Mrs Pepperpot is gone?'

He opened the door into the kitchen; there was the mistletoe hanging over the doorway and, under it, as large as life, stood Mrs Pepperpot!

'Darling husband!' she said, as she put her arms round his neck and gave him a great big smacking kiss:

'Happy Christmas!'

RUTH AINSWORTH

WINKLE AND
THE CHRISTMAS TREE

Tabby Cat and her three kittens slept in a box under the kitchen table. When the kittens grew bigger and their legs became stronger, Tabby Cat sometimes took them for a walk into the dining-room, or the sitting-room, or the hall.

In the dining-room was a gas fire which hissed and had an angry red face. Winkle, who was the bravest of the kittens, hissed back at it.

In the hall was a row of shoes and slippers. The kittens played with the shoe laces and sometimes, when they were tired, they crept into a slipper and fell asleep there because it was so warm and soft, like a cradle.

When it was almost Christmas time, a tall green Christmas tree was brought into the hall, and hung with pretty lights and glass balls and presents done up in gay paper. On the top a Fairy Doll was perched with a silver wand in her hand.

The kittens could do nothing but stare at the beautiful tree.

'May we climb it?' they asked.

'May we bite it?'

'May we lick the candles?'

'Shall we get one of those presents?' they asked.

But Mother Cat's answer to all those questions was 'NO'.

'You may *look*,' said Tabby Cat, 'and that is all. The tree is for the children, not for you. You might, if you were good, have a special present each, but you will find it beside your box when you wake up on Christmas morning.'

Winkle was not content with just looking. He wanted to sniff with his little black nose, and to lick with his small pink tongue, and to touch with his furry paws. So that night, when his two sisters and Tabby Cat were all asleep, he crept softly out of the box and crossed the kitchen floor. He tip-toed into the hall, scrambled up the side of the tub in which the Christmas tree was planted, and began very carefully to climb up.

Climbing was not as nice as he had expected. The branches

of the tree were springy and difficult to cling to, and the thin pointed leaves pricked his nose. His feet caught in the strings of tinsel and paper chains. But he kept on, and at last he reached the top, and found his little damp nose almost touching the golden hair and smooth pink cheeks of the Fairy Doll.

'A happy Christmas!' said the Fairy Doll. 'You are the first kitten who has ever climbed our Christmas tree.'

'A happy Christmas!' replied Winkle. 'You are the first Fairy Doll I have ever spoken to.'

'But you must get down at once, before your mother wakes up and misses you,' said the Fairy Doll. 'Go carefully. You might spoil something if you slipped.'

Winkle went very carefully, but he had to go down head first and that made him feel very dizzy. When he was halfway down, his paws slipped away from a prickly branch. He clutched at a candle to save himself, but the wax was too

smooth and slippery for him to hold. He caught at a string of tinsel for a moment – but the string broke. He leaped at a glass ball and rocked on it till it fell off the tree and smashed on the floor into a thousand splinters.

Winkle fell as well, but he landed on the soft earth inside the tub, and was not hurt.

He picked himself up, and shook himself from his ears right down to the tip of his tail. Then he looked at the broken glass ball. No one could mend it, he was sure. It had been like a lovely shining bubble of a ball. Now it lay on the floor, a thousand jagged scraps of fine glass.

Winkle looked up at the Fairy Doll and mewed sadly:

'Please help me, Fairy Doll! Please help me! Please put the broken ball together again. I know you can with your magic wand. Please try.'

'I will try,' said the Fairy Doll, 'but I don't think I can do anything as difficult as that.'

She spread her fairy wings and flew down from her high branch, and waved her silver wand over the broken glass ball.

Nothing happened.

'Try harder,' mewed Winkle.

'Try harder,' the Fairy Doll whispered to her wand, and she waved it twice.

Still nothing happened.

Then she gave the wand a shake and said crossly:

'You *must* try harder, *much* harder! You must make more magic. You are no better than a clothes' peg.'

The magic wand did not like to be scolded, so the third time the Fairy Doll waved it, it tried very hard indeed, and the tiny glass splinters swept themselves together and made a shining glass ball again, as good as new.

'Thank you, oh, thank you,' purred Winkle, as the Fairy Doll flew up and hung the glass ball in its proper place on the tree.

When the kittens woke up next morning, they found their presents lying on the kitchen rug beside their bed. There was a ping-pong ball for each of them – and what fun they were! The three ping-pong balls rolled all over the floor, and the kittens went chasing after them. Tabby Cat was kept busy hooking them out with her paw from under cupboards and inside the fender.

Winkle never tried to climb the Christmas tree again, but he always waved his tail to the Fairy Doll when he went into the hall, and she waved her wand back. And when he saw the shining glass ball, he purred to himself and thought that that was his secret – his and the Fairy Doll's.

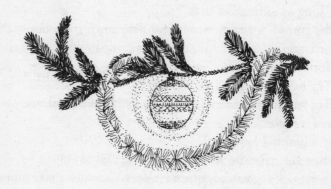

JEAN CHAPMAN

THE WAY OF WISHES

A long time ago it was, and late on Christmas Eve when Farmer Goody and his wife were awakened by a pounding and a thumping on their kitchen door. Two strangers were there, asking for food and shelter for the night.

'Come in! Come in at once!' said Farmer Goody. 'Rest yourselves by the fire.'

'Tomorrow is Christmas,' said Mrs Goody, giving them bowls of soup. 'You must stay and share our Christmas feast.'

The travellers were glad to stay.

The next morning they went with the Goody family to church. There was quite a crowd of them, for the Goody household included lots of children.

Then it was home again to dinner. The children sat close together on a long bench to make room for the two travellers at the table. As far as Christmas dinners go, it didn't seem to be very grand, but it was the best the farm could offer. There was hot roast meat and potatoes, then a big bowl of creamy rice-pudding. The Goody family all ate a little less so that there was plenty for the travellers' plates.

After the meal there was so much laughter and talking and singing that the travellers didn't leave until the next morning. 'I'm glad you stayed,' said Farmer Goody. 'It is a pity that you won't be with us next Christmas.'

'We'll do our best to get here,' said the travellers. 'Thank you, Mrs Goody, we won't forget your good cooking. How many dishes did you serve?'

'Roast meat with potatoes, then creamy rice-pudding,' she said. 'Just the two.'

'Then we'll grant you two wishes,' said one traveller.

'What do you want more than anything in the world?' asked the second.

'That's easy to decide,' said Mrs Goody. 'All we need is food enough to feed our children, and happiness and peace.'

'Your wishes will be granted,' promised the travellers.

They were, too. From that day the farm prospered. The cow had twin calves. The sheep had twin lambs. The pig had so many baby piglets it was hard to count them. And the crops grew better than weeds. Soon people from far and near were talking about the Goody family's fortune.

'It all began when two strangers stayed with us at Christmas time,' Mrs Goody said. 'We hope they will visit us again this coming Christmas. I'll cook a perfect dinner for them then. One to remember. I'll have roast duck and roast pork, cold ham and hot plum pudding, bowls of raisins . . .'

When Farmer Slybones heard the story he told Mrs Goody, 'I do believe your guests were the very same strangers we turned away from our house last year. We feel very badly about it, being Christmas and all. So promise me, Mrs Goody, that you'll send them to my farm when they turn up again.'

'Of course I will,' beamed Mrs Goody. 'I can see that you want to make it up to them because you sent them away.'

And so, when Christmas came again Mrs Goody sent the

travellers to Slybones' Farm, soon after they had arrived at her house. 'We'll be back in the morning to go to church with you,' they promised as they left.

The Slybones had an enormous feast waiting for the travellers. There was ham and bacon. Hot mashed potatoes, cold potato salads, baked potatoes oozing with cheese, and crisp fried potatoes. Long sausages, thin sausages, fat sausages! Juicy pies and hot breads, sliced beetroots and pickled cabbage. There was a big pudding. There were cakes and buns, creamy custards and sweets and nuts and plenty to drink.

It was very late before the travellers could go to bed.

They slept on soft mattresses, under silken sheets and rested their heads on featherdown pillows.

On Christmas morning they rose early to go to church with the Goody family. 'I can't allow you to walk all that way,' objected Farmer Slybones. 'You must take our horses. Ride to church!' He kept urging the travellers to ride to church and almost missed hearing their good-byes. Mrs Slybones tugged at his elbow, and he heard her hissing, 'They haven't asked us how many dishes we ate last night.'

Oh-oh-oh! The travellers were now mounting the horses, but before Slybones had time to be disappointed one of them was calling out, 'That was a magnificent meal last night, Mrs Slybones. Our thanks for it. Tell me now, how many dishes did you serve?'

'Well, let me see . . .' she began putting up her fingers to count them. Slybones quickly pushed her hand away and said quickly, 'Too many for her to count.'

'If that is the case, then we'll grant you four wishes,' said the traveller. 'Two wishes for yourself and two for your wife.'

Well! Before the travellers had gone down the road the

Slybones were quarrelling about the best way to spend the four wishes. She wanted silk and velvet gowns. He wanted more milking cows. She wanted gold bracelets and pearl earrings. He wanted the biggest farm thereabouts. She wanted fur slippers. He wanted . . . oh, there was no end to their wants.

Farmer Slybones became so annoyed he stamped out of the house to do some ploughing. His bad temper brought him more trouble. He was so busy thinking about his wife's silly wishes and wondering how he could make her spend her wishes in *his* way that he drove the horses and plough into a fence. 'Stupid horses!' he shouted. 'Look where you're going! I wish I didn't have to worry about you or the plough!'

Whisk! The horses vanished. The plough vanished. Just disappeared into the air. Gone for ever! Slybones stood alone in the field with his first wish wasted.

Grumbling and growling, he trudged towards his house. Little did he know that his wife was waiting for him at the farmhouse door. She looked this way, that way and then over the fields. 'Where did Slybones get to? He's nowhere to be seen,' she fretted. 'We could use our wishes at once if he were only here. I wish he was here, right beside me now.'

Whizz! And there he was beside her on the doorstep. Mrs Slybones had wasted the second wish, and a noisy argument followed. A shouting, snarling, yelling, roaring, bad-mannered wrangle. Each blamed the other for wasting a wish. He shook his fist. She stamped her feet. The row must have been heard all over the countryside. It was a snip-snap brangle-jangle! Mrs Slybones was so mad she grabbed a plate holding the remains of the Christmas pudding. 'I wish this was on the top of your head!' she screamed.

Squish! The pudding flew off the plate. *Slosh*! It flopped on to Slybones' head. A sprig of holly stuck out of the top. *Slurp*! Soft pudding and brandy sauce slithered into Slybones' ears and eyes. A cherry wobbled to the end of his nose and stuck there.

'Help me! Help me!' he spluttered.

'How? What can I do?' cried his wife.

'Pull the pudding off.'

'It won't come off!' She tried to spoon it off his head, but the pudding stayed stuck.

'Then wash it off.'

'It won't wash off!' She threw a bucket of water over his head, but still the pudding stayed stuck.

'Then cut it off.'

'It won't cut off!' She hacked at the pudding with a knife, but it still stuck.

'Then knock it off.'

'It won't knock off!' She hit the pudding with her rolling-pin. Slybones spun across the room and the pudding stayed stuck just as fast.

'Oh, I wish you'd never made such a soggy pudding,' roared Slybones.

Gerlup! Off came the pudding. Away it went to goodness-

knows-where. Not a crumb was ever seen again. The brandy sauce went with it. So did the cherry from the end of Slybones' nose. And that was the last wish used up. What happened after that no one knows, because the story ends here.

LOTTA'S
CHRISTMAS SURPRISE

'It's funny,' said Lotta, 'how I can do *so* many things!'

She had just let Jonas and Maria hear how well she could whistle, so no wonder she was pleased with herself!

'Come to think of it, I can do everything,' she said.

'So what if you can?' said Maria. 'You certainly boast enough, anyway!'

Jonas was silent for a minute.

'What about slalom skiing then, can you do that?' The only reason he said that was because he was learning how to do it himself. It made Lotta angry.

'Did I *say* I could slalom?' asked Lotta.

'You said you could do everything,' said Jonas.

'And I can too,' said Lotta. 'Everything except slalom.'

'Okay, okay,' said Jonas. And then he and Maria took their skis and went to the big ski slope. Lotta wanted to go skiing too. But not on the big ski slope. I can ski right here in the garden and learn to slalom too, she thought. It can't be very hard. First you go in one direction and then in the other direction, and all the time you wobble your bottom. Anyway, I can wobble my bottom already she thought, trying it to see how good she was.

But before she did any difficult skiing, she wanted to go and see if her mother had anything for her to do. Inside the kitchen, in the yellow house where they lived, Lotta's mother was busy with her Christmas baking. She decorated and kneaded and bustled about in a great hurry. But she smiled when she saw Lotta.

'Lotta, can you take this Christmas loaf round to Mrs Berg?' said Mother, 'and see if you can do anything to help her.'

Lotta was happy to go round to Mrs Berg's house.

'Of course, I can do that *too*. Help people who are ill. I can do everything – almost!'

Mrs Berg lived in the house next door, and just now she wasn't very well. Lotta knew she had something heavy in her chest and she was always out of breath.

'I'm taking Bamsie with me to cheer up Mrs Berg,' said Lotta. Bamsie was an old stuffed pig made of cloth. Lotta had had him since she was little and she still dragged him around everywhere, even though she was a big girl now, over five in fact.

Mother stuffed the loaf into a plastic bag and fastened it with a rubber band.

'Say hello to Mrs Berg for me,' she said, and gave Lotta the bag. 'Come to think of it, you can take the rubbish out at the same time, as you'll be passing the bin.'

'Just give it to me,' said Lotta. 'I'll take care of everything.' Lotta's mother tied up the rubbish bag with a rubber band too. Lying on top was a fish head – they had had kippers for supper the day before, and the fish stared at Lotta through the plastic with horrible white eyes.

'Disgusting,' said Lotta, holding out the bag so Bamsie

could see it too. 'There's a monster in this bag,' she told him. 'But now it's going into the bin, there!'

Then Lotta went out with a bag in each hand and Bamsie under her arm.

Outside the kitchen door were her skis. I'll learn to slalom, thought Lotta, if possible, before Jonas and Maria come home.

'We can slalom over to Mrs Berg's,' she said to Bamsie, stepping into her skis. But Lotta was not used to skiing with two plastic bags *and* Bamsie.

'It won't work,' she said to Bamsie. 'I'll have to stuff you in the bread bag.'

She squeezed him down into the bag and fastened it with the rubber band again. She was sure his eyes looked sadly at her through the plastic.

'It'll only take a minute,' comforted Lotta. 'And if you get hungry, just nibble some bread. But just make sure it doesn't show.'

Then she showed Bamsie how to slalom ski with a plastic bag in each hand.

'First in one direction,' she said, swinging away round the apple tree. 'And then in the other direction,' she said, setting off towards the cherry tree. She wobbled her bottom too, when she remembered to. Sometimes she forgot, but it seemed to work anyway.

Lotta was going very fast. There was a little slope going down to the rubbish bin and she rushed forward extra fast and slowed down at the last minute, just in time to toss the bag in. Then she rushed on. Lotta was out of breath when she reached Mrs Berg's. But not as much as Mrs Berg herself.

Mrs Berg was propped up in bed on her pillows, breathing heavily.

'How's your out-of-breathness?' asked Lotta straight away.

Mrs Berg said it was a little better.

'Lucky for you I came,' said Lotta. 'Guess what I brought you?' She held the bag behind her back so Mrs Berg couldn't see it.

'I wonder what it can be?' said Mrs Berg.

'It's something to eat. It begins with L O, but I'm not saying what it is. You could say it begins with B RRR,' said Lotta, giving Mrs Berg another clue.

'L O and B RRR,' said Mrs Berg. 'No, I can't guess.'

'You can cut it in slices and spread butter on it,' said Lotta. 'I'm not telling you anything else, come on, guess!'

'Lo . . . is it a loaf?' asked Mrs Berg. Lotta laughed.

'Right! and B RRR, that means bread, see?' She held out the bag. But then she let out a scream. There was no loaf in it! 'You horrible monster,' she yelled, as she saw the fishy eyes staring at her through the plastic bag.

'You haven't brought me a monster, have you?' asked Mrs Berg in astonishment. But Lotta was already halfway out of the door . . . Oh, where was her Bamsie? And Mrs Berg's loaf? In the rubbish bin of course! She ran all the way back with a lump in her throat, because she knew just how horrible Bamsie must be feeling down there in the dark, all alone.

'Poor Bamsie,' she said, lifting the lid of the bin. Then Lotta gave a yell that must have been heard by everyone in the street. It was empty! There was no Bamsie and no loaf! Of course, it was Friday. On Fridays, Charlie Fry came with the rubbish truck and emptied all the bins in the street.

'My Bamsie,' screamed Lotta, running down the street.

The rubbish truck was standing down by Larsson's Bakery, and Lotta saw how Charlie Fry had just shoved Larsson's rubbish bag into the huge, open mouth in the back of the truck. Lotta knew there was a kind of mill out the back, which ground up all the rubbish into one big, pulpy mass. Charlie Fry had shown her once.

Lotta screamed! Oh, how she screamed! She knew that that was the end of Bamsie, and now he was just a pulpy mass and not her Bamsie any more.

And it was all her fault!

'What are you yelling about?' asked Charlie.

'My Bamsie,' screamed Lotta. 'You've ground him to bits!'

Charlie was almost as sad as Lotta when he realized what had happened. And Lotta just went on screaming and screaming.

'My Bamsie! My lovely Bamsie!' Then she glared angrily at Charlie, even though it wasn't his fault at all.

'Mrs Berg's loaf, you've ground that up too,' yelled Lotta.

'Loaf?' said Charlie. 'Was it lying on the top in a plastic bag?'

'Yes! And Bamsie too,' shouted Lotta. 'And now he's dead!'

'Yeah, but that's the bag I put on one side,' said Charlie. 'I need bread for my birds.'

Lotta hiccuped then and quietened down. She just stood there feeling butterflies in her tummy, while Charlie went to get the bag from the driver's cab. Imagine if it wasn't the right bag!

But it was.

'I didn't see any Bamsie in it,' said Charlie.

'Didn't you see someone in there with a sad look in his eyes?' asked Lotta. She ripped Bamsie out of the bag and was hugging and kissing him and saying, 'Forgive me, forgive me,' over and over again.

Then suddenly, she saw the other bag that she had thrown on the ground, the one with the monster in it. With a yell she grabbed it and threw it right into the mouth of the rubbish truck.

'Now you'll be a squashed monster,' she said. 'And that suits me fine!'

And then Lotta went back to Mrs Berg's with Bamsie in one hand and the loaf in the other. 'I'm *never* going to learn slalom,' she promised Bamsie. 'That's what caused all this trouble in the first place.'

'Did you leave the loaf somewhere?' asked Mrs Berg, when Lotta came back.

'Oh, no,' said Lotta. 'It's just been on a little trip with my Bamsie.'

And then Mrs Berg had Bamsie in bed with her, while Lotta showed her how good she was at everything. She watered all Mrs Berg's plants, and Scotty, Mrs Berg's snappy little dog, got watered a bit too. And of course he barked at Lotta the whole time. Lotta shook out Mrs Berg's pillows to make them nice and fluffy, and she cut some slices from the loaf and buttered them. She made Mrs Berg eat them because it was good for her out-of-breathness. She washed a few dishes, swept the floor, and even she was amazed at how well she could do everything.

'Of course, it's a lot of hard work,' said Lotta. 'Is there anything else you want me to do?'

'Yes, dear, would you mind running over to the sweet shop to buy me a paper?' asked Mrs Berg. Lotta was quite happy to do that.

'They've got really good sweets there,' she told Mrs Berg.

Mrs Berg gave her the money for the newspaper, and Lotta got a whole ten pence for herself for being such a big help.

'I have to go home for a minute first,' said Lotta, 'because I want to see the Christmas tree that Father's bought. He said he'd have it with him when he came home for lunch.'

But when Lotta walked into the kitchen she was just in time to hear her father's dreadful news.

'There's not a Christmas tree for sale in the whole town,' he said.

Mother was busy making pancakes.

'No Christmas tree,' she said, 'what do you mean? Of course there must be a Christmas tree for sale!' But Lotta's father meant exactly what he said. All the Christmas trees were sold out by the time he came to buy one. Jonas and Maria and Lotta didn't want to believe it.

'We *have* to have a Christmas tree,' said Jonas.

'Have to, have to,' said Father, 'I'm not a magician! I can't do everything.'

'But surely you could have got one before?' said Maria. 'Why didn't you?'

Then Father explained that he always bought the Christmas tree in the big square three days before Christmas. And usually there were plenty of trees to go round. But this year, because of so much snow, it had been hard to bring in enough trees from the forest. In any case, there were none left in the square, and there was nothing he could do.

Jonas looked at Lotta. 'But *you* can,' he said. 'You said you could do everything, Lotta, so get us a Christmas tree!'

'Time to eat,' said Mother.

The family sat down and ate their pancakes in silence, feeling very sad. A Christmas without a Christmas tree, that just couldn't happen!

Then Father had to go back to work.

'I'll search the whole town,' he said. 'If there's a Christmas tree to be had, I'll get it. But if there isn't, then there just isn't.' Then he left.

Jonas and Maria cried. But before Lotta could cry too, she had to go to the sweet shop and buy a paper for Mrs Berg, as she'd promised.

'You can come along,' she said to Bamsie. 'We'll take the toboggan and have some fun, even though we're all miserable.'

It was a downhill stretch all the way to the sweet shop.

'Look out below!' yelled Lotta, and then she was off.

Lotta had to pull the toboggan the last little bit because the sweet shop was beside a service station, and the service station was just off a big main road, where she couldn't go on her toboggan. Mr Blomfield was in charge of the garage, and his wife looked after the shop.

'Hello, little Lotta,' said Mrs Blomfield, 'how are things today?'

'Awful,' said Lotta. 'We're not going to have a Christmas tree this year.'

'That's very sad,' said Mrs Blomfield, 'yes, I heard that all the Christmas trees in town had gone. That's just too sad for words!'

'Yeah,' said Lotta. 'I'm going to cry when I get home.'

But first she bought a paper for Mrs Berg, and then she stood and thought about what kind of sweets she would buy. Liquorice boats, or chocolate, or sherbet drops. These things just couldn't be decided in a hurry.

While Lotta was thinking, something incredible happened. Suddenly, a huge truck came thundering into the service station to fill up, and this particular truck – believe it or not – was loaded with Christmas trees, so high that they had to be piled on top of each other. Lotta went wild when she saw it.

This was no time for thinking about sweets! And how lucky that she hadn't had time to spend her ten pence yet. Surely a Christmas tree couldn't cost more than that!

She rushed over to the driver. He was busy filling his tanks.

'Can I buy a Christmas tree from you?' she asked anxiously. But he didn't even look at her.

'No you can't,' he said, crossly.

'Why?' asked Lotta.

'They're going to New York, every last one of them,' said the driver.

'Why?' asked Lotta.

'Why, why, because they haven't got any Christmas trees there.'

'We haven't got any either,' said Lotta.

'But in New York they'll pay anything for them. Now, out of my way,' said the driver, going to pay Mr Blomfield for the petrol. Lotta ran after him.

'I'll pay anything too!' she screamed with tears in her eyes. 'If I give you ten pence, you can give me a *little* tree, can't you?'

'That's what you think! Out of my way, I said,' said the driver. He didn't want Lotta worrying him. When he had finished paying, he went straight over to his truck, ready to drive off.

But Lotta ran after him.

'Please, please,' she screamed, holding up the ten pence.

''Bye, 'bye, kid,' said the driver, banging the cab door shut. And then he drove off. Lotta cried. She couldn't wait till she got home. It was horrible! A load of Christmas trees driving away like that, and she couldn't even have a little one. Oh, she hated that driver! She glared angrily after him. He had to make a big turn to come out on the road, and look how fast he took the corner! Even Lotta knew he shouldn't drive like that.

Then something more puzzling happened. As the truck roared round the corner one of the trees rolled off the load and landed on the side of the road.

'You dropped a tree,' yelled Lotta. She was always helpful. But the driver neither heard nor saw her. He just drove on. And there stood Lotta watching the tail lights getting smaller and smaller.

Just then Mr Blomfield came out.

'Look, there's a tree lying over there,' said Lotta. 'And I need it. Do you think I dare take it?'

'Well, why not?' said Mr Blomfield. 'It can't just lie there. It's best you take care of it.'

'Well I never . . .' said Mrs Blomfield from the sweet shop. 'Just your luck, Lotta!'

'But what if the driver comes back?' asked Lotta uneasily.

'He'll only have himself to blame,' said Mr Blomfield. 'He shouldn't be throwing his trees around in the first place.'

Lotta thought for a moment. 'Do you want to take my ten pence just to be on the safe side? So *in case* he comes back you can give it to him, okay?'

'Okay,' said Mr Blomfield. 'And if we don't hear from him, you'll get your ten pence back after Christmas.'

The tree was magnificent. Much too big for Lotta to handle. But Mr Blomfield gave her a hand with tying it to the toboggan. Then Lotta arranged a seat for Bamsie right in the middle of some branches.

'The best ride you've ever had,' she said.

''Bye and thanks,' called Lotta. She whistled the whole way. 'Now that's what I call a good whistle,' she said to Bamsie. When Lotta strode into the kitchen at home, she was looking very secretive. But nobody noticed. Jonas and Maria sat in their chairs, crying, and Mother was busy comforting them. No one looked at Lotta.

'What are you two yelling about?' said Lotta.

'Father rang,' said Mother. 'There's not one tree left in the whole town.'

'Strange,' said Lotta. 'Come and see what I've got on my toboggan!'

But Jonas and Maria just went on crying and didn't hear a word Lotta said.

'What a Christmas this is going to be,' said Maria, 'without a tree!'

'Come and see what I've got on my toboggan,' said Lotta again.

'Stop nagging, Lotta,' said Jonas. 'We don't want to look at anything. We're too busy crying.'

'I see,' said Lotta. 'That's a pity, you could have seen a Christmas tree.'

That made Jonas and Maria sit up with a start. 'A Christmas tree, now you're lying again,' said Maria. But they rushed outside with Mother after them. Outside the kitchen door was Lotta's toboggan, and on it was the most beautiful Christmas tree imaginable. And Bamsie was sitting on his branch looking as if he'd just driven the whole load home himself. Jonas and Maria just stared. And Lotta's mother said:

'But, Lotta, where in the world did you get this?'

'Guess!' said Lotta. Then Jonas threw his arms around her and kissed her.

'You were right, Lotta. You really *can* do everything!'

'Didn't I tell you?' said Lotta.

The night before Christmas Eve was tree-decorating night. Everyone helped, Father and Mother and Jonas and Maria and Lotta. And for the tenth time, Lotta told the story about the truck and the driver and everything else.

'We've never had such a beautiful tree,' said Maria. 'Look what magnificent pine needles it's got!'

'And what a lovely smell,' said Jonas.

'And you, dear Lotta,' said Mother. 'This is something

we'll never forget. Imagine, coming home with a Christmas tree for us.'

'No, the Lotta-tree is something we'll remember when all the other trees are forgotten,' said Lotta's father.

Lotta said nothing. She just thought, it's strange, there are so many things I can do. Find Christmas trees and just about *anything*. Yes, in fact I can do *everything*!

Then she looked lovingly at Bamsie who was standing under the tree on his crooked little legs.

'Yes, everything,' she said. 'Except ski with two bags *and* Bamsie!'

ALISON UTTLEY

THE LITTLE FIR-TREE

It was a few days before Christmas, and the Old Grey Woman, who lives in the sky, was busy plucking her geese. The mighty birds lay across her broad knees, and she pulled out the white feathers and scattered them on the earth below.

'Pouf! Away they go! What a litter they make to be sure!' she sighed, and her voice was like the wind howling and moaning far away. Through the air the feathers delicately fluttered, tumbling, tossing, whirling in eddies, and the children looked through their windows and shouted gleefully: 'It's snowing! Look! Snow for Christmas!' and they jumped for joy.

'I told you so,' said their mother. 'I said it would snow. The sky was grey and heavy with the Old Woman up there.'

'Tomorrow we'll play snowballs, and ride in the sledge and make a snowman,' cried the children excitedly, as they went to bed.

Soon the earth was white, covered with the fine feathery mantle thrown down from the sky. The grass and trees felt warm under the snow. In the wood every dark branch was outlined with silver, and every holly leaf held a bunch of snow-flakes in its hollowed green cup. The great beeches spread out their bare boughs and caught the snow in the net of twigs, and the birches stood like frozen fountains, very beautiful.

Near the edge of the wood was a plantation of fir-trees, all very young and small. Their dark outstretched skirts were soon white, so that each tree looked like a little shining umbrella. Now one tree was different from the others, for it possessed a treasure which it held tightly to its heart. It was a nest, which had been built in the spring by a speckled thrush. It was so neat and trim that the fir-tree was very proud of it, and sheltered it with its close thick branches so that no snow fell into it.

The little fir-tree had loved the singing bird which lived there. It had taken care of the eggs and guarded the nestlings from owls and robbers till they were old enough to fly away. It had listened to the thrush's song, and moved its slender branches to the music. When the birds went, the tree waited for them to return or for another bird to come to the empty nest, but the rain fell, and the winds blew, and no bird sat in the home hidden in the heart of the tree.

'Perhaps a winter bird will come, a dazzling white bird, and it will lay eggs of ivory and pearl in my nest,' said the little fir-tree when it saw the snow, but the other trees round it shook their heads till the snow fell in a shower.

'Only hens could do that,' said they, 'and they stay in the farmyards this wintry weather. There will be no bird till next year.'

Then they drooped their branches and waited patiently till they were completely covered up again by the warm white blanket.

In a cottage down the lane lived a little boy and girl. They

made a fine snowman outside their kitchen window, and stuck an old broken pipe of their grandfather's in its wide mouth, and a stick in its hand. They pulled each other up and down the fields in a wooden box, pretending it was a sledge drawn by a pair of fine horses. They made a long slide in the lane, and glided along it, with arms outstretched to the cold air, pretending they were flying birds. They looked at the icy frost-ferns on the windows of the little rooms under the thatched roof, and called them 'Jack Frost's Garden'.

'The children at the castle are going to have a Christmas tree,' proclaimed Peter, pushing his wet red hand into his mother's.

'And it's going to be all a-dazzle with lights and things,' said Sarah.

'Such things are not for us. They cost too much money, but you are going to have a pair of boots a-piece, and that's more useful. Maybe Santa Claus will put something in your stocking, too, if you've been good.' Their mother sighed, knowing how hard it was to manage. She packed them off early to bed, but the grandfather nodded his head and smiled to himself.

On Christmas Eve the old man came into the wood, carrying a spade. He hunted here and there, looking at this tree and that, peering at the colony of firs like a wise owl that wants to find a home. One tree was too big, another too scraggy, another too bushy. Then he saw the little fir-tree, standing like a fairy on one leg, wearing a crinoline of snowy crystals.

'That's the tree! That's the tree for me! Not too big, and not too little, with plenty of close branches, as smooth and round as a bell,' he cried aloud, for like many old people he had a habit of speaking to himself for company.

He shook the snow from the twigs with tender old fingers and then dug round the tree, gathering all the fibrous roots carefully in his hands.

'Oh dear me!' cried the little fir-tree. 'What is going to happen? Do be careful, old man. Don't shake the nest out of my branches!' The sound of its voice was like a sobbing breeze, and the other trees shook their heads and waved their tiny boughs mournfully.

'Good-bye,' they called. 'Good-bye for ever.'

'Whatever happens, I am glad. It's a great adventure,' the little fir-tree sang out bravely, when the old man carried it away.

Across the fields and along the lane it went in the grandfather's warm hands, and the tall trees in the hedgerows looked with pity at it. Little rabbits peeped round the corners of the walls, and a hare stared through a gap to see who was singing the song of the woods. When they saw the fir-tree they nodded and whispered: 'Poor thing! He's caught in a trap!' and they scurried away.

The grandfather walked through a wooden gate, and up the garden path to the cottage door. Then he put the tree in the wood-shed till the children went to bed. He wiped his spade, washed his hands and sat down to tea without saying anything.

At last it was bedtime, and Peter and Sarah had their baths on the kitchen hearth, where a great fire blazed, and sparks flew up the chimney. They sat on their stools and ate their bread and milk, and mince-pie because it was Christmas Eve. Then they each took a candle and trundled up the crooked stair to their little beds, but just as they kissed good night to their mother and grandfather, Peter lifted his head and listened.

'I can hear a little singing noise,' said he. 'What is it?'

Sarah listened too. 'It's only the wind in the wood-shed,' she told her brother, and she ran to tie her stocking to the bedpost, ready for Santa Claus.

When all was quiet upstairs, the grandfather fetched the little tree into the house. The fire crackled, and the tree began to tremble with the heat, so that the twigs rustled and its song died away with fright. 'This is the end,' it thought.

'Here's a little tiddly Christmas tree for Peter and Sarah,' said the old man. 'But take great care of it, for I must put it back in the wood where I found it.'

The mother dropped her sewing and smiled at her father.

'Oh, Grandfather! What a surprise! What a perfect little tree!'

She gazed at the green tree, with its shining branches, to which a powder of snow still clung. There was something particularly beautiful about this tree, fresh from its dreams in the wood. As for the little fir-tree, it plucked up its courage and stared round the room, at the table with the bread and cheese, and the cat on the hearth, and the china dogs on the mantelpiece, and the holly wreath over the loud-ticking clock.

'There's a nest in it,' went on the grandfather, proudly. 'Peter will like that,' and he showed the mother the neat round nest hidden under the branches.

'Now I'm going out to buy some things to hang on it, so that it will be as fine as the tree up at the castle. You plant it carefully all ready for me!' He reached up to the teapot on the mantelpiece, the lustre teapot which was his money-box, and took out some coins.

'I'm going to be extravagant for once, for I've got a bit of my pension left,' he laughed, and he set off down the dark lanes to the village shop.

While he was away, the mother planted the tree in plenty of soil in the big earthenware breadmug which stood in the corner of the room, stocked with her home-made loaves. The bread she placed in a row on the dresser, small round cobs, each with a cross on the top in memory of the Christ Child, and the tree she dragged to the middle of the room, near the lamp and her sewing. As her needle went in and out she heard a tiny singing sound, and she knew it was the happy tree chanting its woodland song.

After some time the old man came back with a brown paper parcel and bulging pockets. From the parcel he took little red and blue and gold balls to hang on the tree, and a silver glass trumpet, and four tiny coloured glass bells with little clappers which tinkled like icicles. He had a box of silver tinsel tassels to droop from the boughs like falling water, and a couple of golden roses. He brought from his pockets two oranges, and three rosy apples, and a couple of tiny baskets of almond fruits. The mother and the old man hung them all about the tree, so that it looked as if the little glossy fir-tree had stepped straight out of fairyland.

On the tip-top of the tree's head, the grandfather's shaking fingers fastened a little Dutch doll with a wisp of tinsel round her waist, a midget of a doll as big as his thumb-nail, and in the nest he placed a lovely glass bird, with a white body and feathery tail and a silver beak and wings.

The tree quivered with delight, so that all the bells began to ring, and all the balls and sparkles jumped up and down and gleamed in the firelight. At last a bird had come to live in the nest again, a winter bird, snow-white like the frosty earth!

Throughout Christmas Eve the tree stayed in the quiet room, listening to the ticking of the clock, and the chink, chink of the dying fire, and the chirrup of the cricket which lived under the hearthstone, and the tree, too, murmured and rustled its branches, waiting for the glass bird to chirp and sing.

Then dawn came, and the mother made the fire again, so that the lights sprang out and the tree's dark branches reflected the glow. The kettle sang, the blue cups and saucers were placed with their tinkling spoons on the clean white cloth, and the bacon hissed in the frying-pan.

Suddenly there was a patter of feet, and a sound of laughter on the stairs. The door burst open and the two children came running in, carrying bulging little stockings in their hands.

'A Merry Christmas! A Merry Christmas!' they cried, hugging their mother and grandfather. Then they saw the

pretty tree standing as demure as a little girl in her first party frock, and they gave a shout.

'A Christmas tree! Where did it come from? Oh! How lovely! It's a real live one, growing.'

'There's a teeny, tiny doll on the top. Is it for me?' asked Sarah.

'There's a real nest,' exclaimed Peter, 'and there's a bird in it, too.' They both danced round the tree singing:

> Christmas comes but once a year,
> And when it comes it brings good cheer.

'Just see if that bird has laid any eggs,' said the smiling old grandfather, and when Peter slipped his hand in the thrush's nest he found two silver sixpences!

That was a day for the fir-tree to remember. Never as long as it lived would it forget that day! It stood, the centre of the festivities, watching the Christmas games, listening to the Christmas songs, humming softly to the bells from the church across the village green.

'Can't you hear it?' whispered Peter. 'The tree is singing.' But Sarah said it was only the wind through the keyhole, for trees never sang.

In a few days the grandfather took the fir-tree back to the wood, with the nest safe and sound under the branches. He uncovered the hole, and planted the roots deep in it, so that the tree stood firmly among its companions.

'Tell us again,' cried the fir-trees in the plantation, when the little tree had told its story for the hundredth time. 'Did you say a snow-white bird came to live in your nest? Did you have bells on your boughs? And gold roses? Tell us again.'

So once more the fir-tree told the story of Christmas.

'But the bird never sang at all,' it added. 'I shall be glad to see my thrush again next spring. The bells were not as sweet-sounding as the bluebells in the wood, and the roses had no scent at all. But it was a beautiful Christmas, and I was very, very happy!'

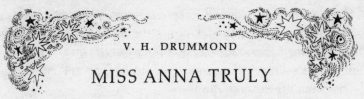

V. H. DRUMMOND

MISS ANNA TRULY
AND THE CHRISTMAS LIGHTS

'I hate washing up,' said Miss Anna Truly.

'So do I,' said Mrs Truly.

'So do I,' said Farmer Truly.

It was the week before Christmas at the Truly Farm.

'Wouldn't it be lovely if Santa Claus brought us a washing-up machine for Christmas?' remarked Anna.

They all laughed.

'Not likely,' sighed Farmer Truly.

Just then John Purse, the son of a farmer who lived nearby, came to the door.

'Can I take Anna to the Great City to see the Christmas lights?' he asked.

Anna's parents agreed, providing he brought her back in time for supper.

As John and Anna ran to the Railway Station it started to snow. They bought return tickets and jumped on to a fast train.

When they arrived in the Great City, the Ticket Collector said, 'This train will return to the country in one hour's time. NO train later!'

John gasped. 'It won't be dark then. The Christmas lights won't be lit.'

'Never mind,' said the Ticket Collector. 'Why don't you go and see Santa Claus in Magnum's, the big store? It's over there – with the Christmas Tree and huge candles on the porch.'

'That's a marvellous idea,' exclaimed John and Anna, and they ran off through the snow.

Inside Magnum's they saw a notice: SANTA CLAUS IN TOYLAND . . . GROUND FLOOR.

On the way to Toyland, they came to the moving stairs . . . one going up . . . one going down.

'Let's play on these,' said John. 'It would be tremendous fun!'

Anna was rather frightened of the moving stairs. They seemed to move mysteriously and to make strange sounds. She was reluctant to put her toes on to them.

'We'll stand and watch until you get used to them,' said John.

So they watched the people going up the stairs, and then they watched the people coming down. Then Anna noticed a red button on the banister beside the stairs. She gave it a push.

At once the moving stairs stopped moving! There was a sudden silence, and then all the customers gave a great cry.

'The moving stairs have stopped! Have STOPPED!'

The customers gasped and pointed. Luckily there was no one on the steps.

The Store Manager came running up. He sent a message to the Engineer, who soon made the stairs move again. But he was furious as he turned to the customers.

'Who did it?' he cried angrily. 'Who pressed the red emergency button that stopped the moving stairs?'

'I did,' said Anna bravely. 'I didn't know that it was an emergency button.'

'It's an offence to push the red button except in an emergency,' said the Store Manager. 'You must pay a penalty.'

'We can't pay,' said John. 'We have no money.'

At this the Store Manager grabbed hold of them, saying, 'Then I shall imprison you both in my office until your relations come and bail you out.'

Just then a voice came over the loud speaker: 'Attention everyone. Attention please! There is a thief in the building. Vilewort the Villain has stolen a bag of money from the Chief Cashier's desk. He is wearing a black bowler hat, black gaiters, and a black moustache. Anyone who sees Vilewort the Villain, kindly inform the Management at once.'

'How dreadful!' cried the Store Manager hysterically. 'I must call the Police immediately!'

He let go of John and Anna, and rushed off. The customers started looking everywhere for Vilewort.

'Quick, Anna,' said John, 'we'll escape!'

At that moment a man appeared at the top of the stairs. He was wearing a black bowler hat, black gaiters, a black moustache . . . and he was carrying a big cash bag . . .

'Crick-a-crick, crick-a-cree, you can't catch me!' he cried as he started down the moving stairs.

It was Vilewort the Villain. But Anna kept her head.

Once more, she pressed the red button.

The moving stairs stopped so suddenly that Vilewort stumbled and was flung into the air. Over and over he turned until he fell with a crash on to the floor, the cash bag on top of him.

At once John sat on Vilewort's head and Anna rushed to hold his feet.

'Get off my head! Let go of my feet!' he shouted.

But John and Anna were brave. They did not move.

At that moment, Mr Magnum himself, the owner of Magnum's Store, appeared. He was easy to recognize because, being so very important, he always wore a top hat, even indoors. 'Why are you sitting on that gentleman's head?' he asked John.

'It's the thief,' gasped John.

Vilewort the Villain was wriggling dreadfully and kicking out at Anna. John was afraid he was going to escape.

'How did you catch him?' asked Mr Magnum.

'It was Anna. She pushed the red button,' said John; and he described the fall of Vilewort.

Then the Store Manager arrived with a Policeman.

The Policeman said, 'Well done! You have caught the worst villain in the land.'

Then he put hand-cuffs on to Vilewort, and marched him off to the Police Station.

When the stairs were moving again, the Store Manager picked up the cash bag to take back to the Chief Cashier.

The customers began to shout: 'Hurrah! Hurrah! Hurrah for the brave children who caught Vilewort the Villain.'

'Will you come with me to Toyland?' Mr Magnum said to Anna and John. 'I would like to give you each a present . . . a big present . . . an electric train . . . an aeroplane . . . a doll's house . . . a bicycle . . . a tricycle . . . anything you like!'

Anything they liked! The children could hardly believe their ears.

'But first let us go up the moving stairs . . . just for fun!' said Mr Magnum.

'Yes, let's,' cried John.

Anna was not a bit nervous with Mr Magnum holding her hand. They went all the way up to the top of the store – five flights – and then all the way down again to Toyland.

Santa Claus was standing at the entrance to Toyland with his sleigh and Rosie the Reindeer. He greeted them cordially.

It took them a long time to walk round Toyland.

Suddenly John spotted something he had always wanted . . . a bicycle! When Mr Magnum said he could have it, John thanked him many times.

'Now what would *you* like?' Mr Magnum asked Anna. 'Remember, it must be a *big* present.'

So Anna said, 'Then I would like a washing-up machine, please . . . for my mother and father and me. We hate washing up.'

'So do I,' said Mr Magnum. 'But we must go to another department.' Then, as they were leaving, he picked up a beautiful doll from a chair, saying, 'And you shall have this too.'

'Oh, thank you, thank you,' cried Anna delightedly.

The doll was wearing nylon underclothes and could open and shut her eyes and walk about.

Suddenly all the customers ran toward the windows. 'The lights!' they cried. 'The Christmas lights have come on!'

'Oh, it must be very late,' John cried in alarm. 'We've missed the last train. Farmer Truly will be very cross.'

'Don't worry,' said Santa Claus. 'Rosie and I will take you home on our sleigh. Where do you live?'

'Truly Farm,' said Anna gratefully.

'I know it well,' said Santa Claus.

'May I come too?' asked Mr Magnum. 'Just for the ride.'

'Delighted,' said Santa Claus.

John clutched his bicycle, and Anna her doll, as they all trotted off through many departments of Magnum's Store.

When they reached the Electrical Department they stopped so that Mr Magnum could choose a magnificent washing-up machine, and then he and Santa lifted it on to the back of the sleigh.

Then they climbed into the sleigh with their presents, and Rosie the Reindeer trotted them out through the main door. It had stopped snowing.

Anna gazed with delight at the glittering decorations and the sparkling snow.

'We are seeing the Christmas lights after all,' she whispered to John.

Every street they sped through was brilliantly lit with coloured lights and different decorations.

When they had left the shopping centre, Anna said to Santa Claus: 'Now can we fly please?'

'I never fly before Christmas Eve,' said Santa Claus. 'That would be reckless behaviour.'

Soon they came to the City Square, where the largest Christmas Tree in the world was standing. But there was a tremendous traffic jam round the City Square.

So . . . Santa Claus decided that they should fly after all! 'Rosie's magic bells help her to rise,' he explained.

He waved his whip and called to Rosie: 'Swish your tail! Quiver your antlers! Lift your feet! And . . . Fly! Fly! FLY!'

On the last *fly*, Rosie soared into the air above all the cars and buses. People stuck in the traffic jam looked up at them with envy.

They flew over the largest Christmas Tree in the world and saw the carol singers round it, singing loudly.

'Boom! Boom! One . . . two . . . three . . . four . . . five . . . six,' said the great clock, Big Alice, as they passed her lighted face.

'Oh dear, it's getting late,' said John.

'Don't worry,' said Santa Claus. 'Look . . . there's the open country ahead.'

They flew over the snow-covered countryside until they saw Truly Farm below.

'Rosie, descend,' commanded Santa Claus.

Rosie circled round the farm and made a graceful landing. Then she rushed in through the front door.

Imagine how surprised Farmer and Mrs Truly were to see a reindeer rushing into their kitchen. And they were even more astonished to see Anna and John sitting with Mr Magnum and Santa Claus in the sleigh behind her.

When they had heard all the adventures and seen the magnificent presents, and placed the washing-up machine in a suitable position, Mrs Truly asked Santa Claus and Mr Magnum to stay to supper.

'I am afraid we have only got fish toes to eat,' she said.

'I have never tasted fish toes,' said Mr Magnum. 'I would love to try them.'

So they all sat down to a meal of fried fish toes and chips. Rosie lay in front of the fire. She declined the fish toes that were offered to her.

'These fish toes are delicious,' exclaimed Mr Magnum.

John said, 'When Anna and I grow up we are going to get married, and every Christmas I will take her to the Great City to see the Christmas lights.'

'And Rosie and I will bring you home,' said Santa Claus.

'I will look forward to that,' said Anna.

After supper, everyone thanked everyone.

Then Rosie took Mr Magnum and Santa Claus along the snowy roads, back to the Great City; and John rode away on his beautiful new bicycle.

'No more horrid washing up,' said Miss Anna Truly as she helped put the dirty dishes into the magnificent washing-up machine.

BEATRIX POTTER

WAG-BY-WALL

Once upon a time there was an old woman called Sally Benson who lived alone in a little thatched cottage. She had a garden and two fields, and there was grazing for a cow on the bog in summer while the fields were shut off to grow hay grass.

While her husband was alive, and able to work, they had lived comfortably. He worked for a farmer, while Sally milked the cow and fed their pig at home. After Sally became a widow she had a hard struggle. Tom Benson's long illness had left debts.

The cottage had belonged to Sally's mother, and to her grandparents before her. Her grandfather had been a cattle dealer. He bought and sold cattle at fairs, and made a bit of money. Nobody knew what he had done with it. He did not seem to spend much; and he never gave away one farthing. The old furniture was poor and plain; the only handsome piece that had belonged to the old man was 'Wag-by-wall' the clock. 'Tick: tock: gold: toes: tick: tock: gold: toes;' it repeated over and over; till anybody might have felt provoked to throw a shoe at it – 'Tick: tock: gold: toes:'

Sally took no notice. The clock had been saying those words ever since she was born. Nobody knew what it meant. Sally thought the world of the clock; and she loved her old singing kettle. She boiled water in it to make balm tea. She made it in a jug, and she grew the lemon-scented balm in her own garden. The kettle had been cracked and mended more than once.

The last time Sally took it to the smithy, Isaac Blacksmith looked at it over his spectacles and said – 'More patch than bottom. It will cost you more than a new kettle.' 'Nay, nay! thou mun patch it, Isaac Blacksmith! I tell thee, thou mun patch it, and thou mun patch it again!' Sally stood on tiptoes to whisper – 'I tell thee – it can sing.' 'Aye, aye? like a toom barrel?' said Isaac Blacksmith, blowing the bellows.

So Sally went on using her old kettle, and it sang to her. The kettle sang on the hearth, and the bees sang in the garden, where she grew old-fashioned flowers as well as potatoes and cabbages. There were wallflowers, pansies and roses in their season; balm for her own herb tea; and thyme, hyssop and borage that the honey bees love.

When Sally sat knitting by the cottage door she listened to the bees – 'Arise – work – pray: Night follows day: Sweet Summer's day.' The bees hummed drowsily amongst the flowers – 'To bed with sun: day's work well done.' The bees went home into their hives at dusk.

Presently, indoors, the kettle began to sing; at first it sang gently and slowly, then faster and faster and more loud, as it came to boiling and bubbling over. It sang words something like this – to the tune of 'Ash Grove' –

'With pomp, power and glory the world beckons vainly,
    In chase of such vanities why should I roam?
While peace and content bless my little thatched cottage,
    And warm my own hearth with the treasures of home.'

Sally Benson sitting by her fire on a winter's evening
listened to the song of the kettle and she was contented. The
cottage was warm and dry; it was whitewashed within and
without, and spotlessly clean. There was no upstairs; only the
kitchen, with cupboards and a box bed in the wall; and behind
the kitchen was another tiny room and a pantry. Sally
thought it was a palace; she had no wish to live in a big house.
    Above the kitchen hearth at the south end of the cottage,
there was a tall stone chimney stack standing up above the

roof. Dry thatch is dangerous for catching fire from sparks, but there was plenty of green moss and house leek growing beside Sally Benson's chimney. Under the same long low roof at the north end was a wood shed.

A pair of white owls lived in the shed. Every summer, year after year, they nested there – though it could scarcely be called a 'nest'. The hen owl just laid four eggs on a bare board under the rafters. The little owlets were like balls of fluff, with big dark eyes. The youngest owlet, that hatched out of the last laid egg, was always smaller than the other three. Sally called him Benjamin.

When the little owlets were old enough to come out, they climbed up the thatch and sat in a row on the ridge of the roof. They hissed and craned their necks, and twisted their heads to watch their parents, mousing over the bog. The old owls flitted noiselessly over the coarse grass and rushes; they looked like great white moths in the twilight.

As the young owlets grew older, they became more and more hungry – the mother owl used to come out hunting food by daylight in the afternoons. The pee-wits over the bog swooped at her, crying and wailing, although she only sought for mice. Little breezes stirred the cotton grass; and Nancy Cow, knee deep in sedge and meadow-sweet, blew warm breath lazily. Her big feet squelched amongst moss and eyebright and sundew; she turned back to firm turf and lay down to wait until Sally's voice called her home for milking.

When the old owls brought back mice they fed each wide gaping mouth in turn. Amongst the jostling and hissing and snatching, Benjamin was often knocked over. Sometimes he rolled down the thatch and fell off the roof. Sally picked him up and put him back. If the night had been wet she dried him by the fire. One morning she found all four baby owlets on the doorstep hissing at the cat.

Sally was very fond of the owls. Indeed she was fond of all things; a smiling friendly old woman with cheeks like withered apples.

But 'good times and hard times – all times go over'. While the hard times lasted they hit poor Sally very hard. There came a year of famine. Rain spoilt the hay and harvest, blight ruined the potato crop. Sally's pig died, and she was forced to sell her cow to pay the debts. There seemed to be nothing for it but to sell the cottage also, and end her days in the Poor House. She had nobody that she could turn to, no one to ask for help.

She and Tom had lost their only child – a daughter. Such a dear pretty girl she had been, with yellow curls, rosy cheeks, and blue eyes always laughing, until she ran away to marry a wastrel. Sally had sent money when a baby girl was born – another little 'Goldie-locks'. Time and again they wrote for money. When Sally had no more to send them they faded out of sight.

On Christmas Eve Sally Benson sat by the fire reading a letter, which the postman had brought her. It was a sad letter, written by a stranger. It said that her daughter and her son-in-law were dead, and that a neighbour – the writer – had taken in their child into her home out of pity. 'A bonny child she is; a right little Goldie-locks; eight years old, and tidy and helpful. She will be a comfort to her Grannie. Please send money to pay her fare, and I will set her on her way. I have five mouths to feed so I cannot keep her long. Please send money soon, Mrs Benson.' Poor Sally! with no money and no prospect but the Poor House.

That Christmas Eve in the moonlight, a white owl sat on the chimney stack. When a cloud came over the moon, the owl dozed. Perhaps a wisp of blue smoke floating upwards made him sleepy – he swayed forward and fell into the chimney.

Down below Sally Benson sat by the hearth, watching the dying fire. One hand crumpled the letter in the pocket of her old black skirt; the other thin trembling hand was twisted in her apron. Tears ran down her poor old nose; she mopped them with her apron. She was not crying for her daughter whose troubles were over. She was crying for little Goldie-locks. She sat on and on, into the night.

At length there was a noise high up in the chimney. There came a rush of soot and stones; small stones and mortar came first. Several large heavy stones tumbled after; and the white owl on the top.

'Save us! What a dirty mess!' said Sally, scrambling to her feet and forgetting her troubles. She picked up the owl gently, and blew the soot off him, and set him on a chair. The soft feather tip of one wing was scorched; otherwise he was unhurt. But the soot had got into his eyes and his gullet; he blinked and gasped and choked. Sally fetched a drop of milk and fed him with a spoon.

Then she turned to sweep up the mess on the hearth. There was a smell of charred wood and burning wool. Amongst the stones was a black thing which smoked. It was an old stocking tied round the ankle with a bit of string. The foot was full of something heavy. Gold showed through a hole in the toes. 'Tick: tock: gold: toes:' said Wag-by-wall the clock.

Something seemed to have happened to Wag-by-wall; he went whirrr, whirra, whirr! trying to strike. When he

struck at last he struck 14 instead of 12; and he changed his tick. Instead of saying 'Tick: tock: gold: toes: tick: tock: gold: toes!' he said 'Tick:er:tocks:Goldie:locks:tick:er:tocks: Goldie:locks,' and those were his words ever after.

Sally Benson fetched her little granddaughter to live with her. She bought another cow, and a pig, and she grew potatoes and balm and sweet flowers in her garden for the honey bees. And every summer the white owls nested in the wood shed.

Sally enjoyed a cheerful contented old age, and little Goldie-locks grew up and married a young farmer. They lived happily ever after, and they always kept the singing kettle and Wag-by-Wall the clock.